Girl Seeking Farm

A FINDING HOME NOVEL

HANNAH DOVE

PLOTWORKS PUBLISHING

ISBN (electronic): 978-1-960936-27-1

ISBN (print): 978-1-960936-28-8

Contents

Dedication

For anybody who keeps the memory of a farm deep down inside
—you know who you are.

Chapter One

THE MAN JESSICA used to love was standing in front of the judge, his head held a little too high, his chin tipped up a little too proudly.

He was wearing a gray Brooks Brothers suit with an old-fashioned cut, the high-waisted pants, trim jacket, barest hint of a pocket square, and a silver pin punched through his necktie. A small smirk resided at the corner of his mouth.

"Do you have anything left to say before I read the sentence?" said the judge. He was looking at the defendant over the tops of his spectacles. His eyes were two pieces of red-hot charcoals.

As Jessica waited for the response, she felt the tears starting to well in her eyes. She knew that he wasn't a bad man. Or, more precisely, that while he may have done some bad things, he was still essentially good. There was no doubting that—not to her, not right now.

A moment earlier, however, the judge had found him guilty of a slew of charges related to high finance. He'd used the words *insider trading*.

"This is your last chance," said the judge.

The man Jessica used to love threw his head back. "I'm innocent of all charges," he said, "and I will be vindicated."

Jessica smiled. She still admired his confidence. That had been the very quality that had drawn her towards him the very first time they'd locked eyes at the midtown Manhattan watering hole, across the brass fixtures and recessed lighting and expensive cocktails. He hadn't delayed either, heading straight over the moment he saw her moisten her lips.

She definitely hadn't complained.

It was an instant attraction. The lovemaking had come fast and furious, and even despite his long hours at a major investment house, she'd turned into a willing servant, in a way she never had before, ready to skitter over to his minimalist condo at a moment's notice.

There was a lot that she didn't know about him, and that was mostly because of his schedule. As far as she could tell, he had worked twelve to fourteen hours a day, nearly every day, for eight months. She didn't think that was really possible, but she was willing to tolerate the ambiguity. Six feet something, a full head of thick hair, gleaming white teeth, a row of dapper suits in his closet, the occasional phone call whose timing was impossible to predict, the mischievous eyes that always seemed distracted, that never told the full story ... he was a catch. He knew it too.

But he wasn't the marrying kind.

Everyone Jessica knew had told her so. They had all said he *wasn't* worth it, that he *wasn't* husband material, wasn't the type of man you kept at the top of your contacts list on your phone.

Once ensnared, however, she'd found herself helpless to change. And now here she waited, in the spectator seats of a courtroom, staring at the coffered ceiling high above her face, tears in her eyes, waiting for the judge's pronouncement.

Two seats away, a thin blonde woman in an expensive

cream-colored suit sat alone. Her face was classically beautiful, rouged and powdered. A pair of expensive bracelets dangled from her thin wrists.

Jessica noticed that she was clutching a small napkin. And that it was sweat-soaked.

"I would like to say," he continued, "that this entire case has rested on fraudulent evidence and falsified testimony. I am the *victim* here."

He looked around the room. She'd heard him say this a dozen times already, spoken casually to colleagues on the phone, muttered into his glass of whiskey, shouted out to the twinkling city lights from his balcony. She'd obediently followed him around, playing the dutiful wife, agreeing with him.

But Jessica *wasn't* his wife. And, deep down, in her heart of hearts, she'd known that she never would be.

The judge shrugged. "Is that all?"

"Yes, your honor."

The judge cleared his throat. "Hearken now to the sentence the court imposes upon you. On counts one, two, and three the court sentences you to four years in prison. That's a total of twelve years, to be served in a minimum security federal prison. This is a sentence that is provided by our statutes. It is a fair and just and righteous sentence. Custody, Mister Officer. Stand down."

He banged the gavel. The man Jessica used to love didn't crack. He just stood there, stock still, as though he were an actor in a play that he didn't realize had just ended.

A bailiff placed a pair of handcuffs upon him, turned him sideways, and began marching him towards the side door of the courtroom. The smirk remained pasted on his face.

Jessica's shoulders slumped. Deep down, she'd known this was coming. She'd prepared herself for this moment for weeks, but she still felt swept away by the power and the finality of the court's ruling.

Then, as though propelled by somebody else, she stood up and reached out over the railing.

"Don't go," she said, "I need you."

His eyes landed upon Jessica. Then she pulled back as she saw something she didn't recognize, something cold and ancient. It was *remorselessness*, the flat stare of the unempathetic. She may as well be looking into the eyes of a reptile.

And as he swept by her, she suddenly knew that everybody had been right, that he really *hadn't* been the right man, that he would eat his own young if it suited him.

And that scared her.

Jessica had been ready to fight for him, to defend him, to make jailhouse visits for him, to wait for him as long as necessary until his sentence had been finished. Twelve years wasn't really that long to wait. She'd still be fertile by the time he got out.

But that cold look in his eye... *It didn't feel right.* Jessica felt like she'd been climbing a ladder to a gorgeous future only to discover that the ladder had been leaning against the wrong wall.

And then—

—she watched him walk past her outstretched arms—

—and straight to the blonde woman with the thin wrists.

He kissed the woman on the cheek, murmured a few words. The blonde woman nodded, looking like she was steeling herself.

Then Jessica noticed, on the long and delicate fourth finger of her left hand, a wedding ring. It had a diamond the size of a bouillon cube.

Jessica collapsed in her seat, feeling the wind knocked out of her.

Of course he'd been married.

Of course.

She watched the bailiffs push the man she used to love through the side door. She watched the side door close.

Then it was over.

The other spectators around her stood up, stretched. Jessica stayed in her seat, legs trembling, wondering exactly how and why she had gotten so emotionally wound up with this financier, how she could've been so blind as to see that the high-rise condo was only *one* of his homes. And that she had, most likely, been just one of many side women.

Jessica squeezed her hands into fists. She felt used, stupid, and furious.

She was better than that. She vowed to *never* let this happen again.

Never.

The judge banged the gavel. The spectators stood up. Someone muttered something about getting what he deserved.

Jessica barely heard any of it. She was floating towards the exit, past the blonde wife with the expensive jewelry on the thin wrists, past the solitary news camera, out into the fresh air—

—feeling as though she were awakening from a long, restless sleep.

Chapter Two

AS JESSICA STARED at the hideous feathered heel in her hand, she vowed to find the interior decorator who'd overnighted this Frankenstein to her desk.

She was a year and a half into an editorial internship at a fashion magazine called *Spretza*. The publication, which dedicated itself to chronicling all things Italian and expensive on the island of Manhattan, had been teetering on the brink of bankruptcy, thanks to continuously shrinking advertising money. The monthly magazine was at least thirty pages thinner now than it had been when Jessica began.

Her first task every day was simple: She had to unpack the garbage barge. That was her derisive nickname for the wheeled canvas cart that was delivered to her basement workspace every morning. It was filled with UPS boxes sent to the magazine by designers hoping for exposure for their products.

Inside those boxes were high heels.

When she'd first started, Jessica had been over the moon, delirious with happiness. Arriving at work every day, she'd ripped into the delivery cart with gusto, exploring the new goods. It felt like Christmas morning every day. She'd opened, examined, and giggled at thirty new high heels each day, all before ten o'clock am.

Now, a year later, that bloom was definitely off the rose.

Jessica had discovered that wading through the slush pile in any industry was a scut job, one step removed from cleaning bathrooms. She'd learned the bitter irony that none of the shoes sent to *Spretza* were ever considered for publication by the executive editor. To make a name, an unknown young designer needed a powerful and established ally in the world of fashion.

Jessica certainly wasn't that person. She was an unknown girl toiling down here in the sequin mines.

She sighed, trying to remember why, once upon a time, she'd wanted this job so badly. It probably had something to do with Carrie Bradshaw. Or Bridget Jones. Or the six goofy members of *Friends*. Or any other filmed entertainment that had tricked her into thinking that moving to New York City and working at a fashion magazine was the end-all-be-all of life.

A scowl came over her face. She didn't *like* feeling this way. But she did, and the pieces of her world were starting to break up like an ice floe.

She looked at the feathered heel. It was oddly shaped, with pink feathers, silver glitter, and a turquoise flower glued right over the toes. Tacky didn't even come close to describing it.

"Phineas," she said, "can you tell me why this looks so bad?"

"Because it's ugly as hell," said her coworker without even glancing.

The voice belonged to Phineas Washington. He was a paid intern in the art department by day, a renegade cartoonist by night, and fabulously weird at all times. He'd become, by default, her best friend in New York. Before arriving in the city, she hadn't known that you could even *have* gay best friends, but she and Phineas had been each other's support system for over a year now. They looked out for one another at *Spretza*, a place where slings and arrows rained down from every quarter, where ambition and treachery were practically added to the water.

"I want your honest opinion," she said. "This is from a so-called designer."

"Who's obviously trying to make a buck," replied Phineas. He was wearing a bowtie, a tweedy sport coat, and a pencil mustache. It was his look of the week. Last week he'd been into choirboy chic, cloaking himself in white robes and carrying a hymnal. The week before that, he'd been a Prussian military officer.

"Isn't everybody?" she said.

Phineas scratched his mustache with a finger. "He's aiming low. Pandering. Mass over class."

"I really don't like it."

"That doesn't matter," he said. "Jessica, if *you* don't like something, guaranteed that fifty percent of the population *will*. And by the way, that's a compliment."

"Thank you," she said. Then she chucked the heel into the discard bin that she kept behind her standing desk. Phineas lunged for it. "Hey, don't throw it *out*. The Grand Duchess can wear it."

Jessica smiled. The Grand Duchess was Phineas' potbellied pig. She and Jessica had a checkered history, mostly because the pig had once eaten Jessica's entire makeup case.

"You're seriously going to put one high heel on a pig?" she said.

"No," replied Phineas, as though it were the most obvious thing in the world, "I'm going to *feed* her from it. She's very particular about the look of her trough."

He saw Jessica staring at him.

"You're not understanding me," he said.

"I *never* understand you."

"Well, if you stopped sleeping with half of Manhattan, you might get some brain cells back."

She shot an evil stare at him. "Why do you like to torture me so much?"

"Because it's easy."

"Apologize."

"No."

"Say I'm sorry."

"I'm sorry you're such a slut."

Jessica threw a pencil at him. That wasn't true at all, and Phineas knew it, which is why he was teasing her. Not counting the newly-jailed financier, Jessica had actually been quite chaste during her year and a half in the city, at least compared with most of her girlfriends. She'd never felt comfortable giving herself over fully to a strange man. The timing had to be just right, the man just mysterious enough, the emotions just calibrated enough—and those things rarely coincided.

Jessica slumped on a stool. "I don't get it. I'm supposed to be roaring with ambition right now, trying to rise up the journalistic ladder."

"A plot that's been drilled into you by a thousand chicklit books," answered Phineas.

She moodily chewed on a fingernail. "I just wonder if that's me."

"Keep talking," said Phineas. "This sounds like a process of discovery."

"This magazine promised me a promotion in six months."

"And?"

"It's been over a year." She dumped another set of heels out of a box and kicked the cardboard against the back wall.

"So."

"So this isn't what I'd expected."

"It's exactly what *I'd* expected."

"Well, you're doing art. That's your skill set."

"What's your skill set?"

"I don't know. And I'm waiting for a promotion that may never come."

"For a job that you need to be a sociopath to keep," he added.

"True."

Jessica looked over at his screen. Phineas was doing a mockup of page thirty-four of next month's issue.

"Is that *layout*?"

"You bet your little Bible-loving tush it is."

"Who let you do that?"

"Nobody *let* me. I'm just *doing* it. Now, whether they decide to use it is up to them. Someone's going to notice that they've got goddamned Picasso down here in the dungeon."

"Picasso going through his gay period."

"Better stay off the period jokes," he shot back. "I've got *your* monthly schedule marked on my calendar so I know *exactly* when to call in sick."

Jessica grinned and turned back to her computer. Then her phone began to ring in her purse.

She frowned. She'd sworn that she'd set it on silent.

Picking it up, she saw the caller ID ... and gasped.

It read *Nonna*.

That was her grandmother. But Nonna never called her, *never*, unless there was a specific reason. She saw no reason to chat, since she viewed phone calls as interruptions to her daily chores on the farm.

"Nonna?" said Jessica, answering.

At the other end, a male voice cleared his throat. "No, it's Young Billy."

That was one of the three workers on the farm. Young Billy was a lifer, a dependable part of her grandmother's property, a man who knew a lot about cattle and crops and who didn't mind working fourteen hours a day. He was nearly fifty years old now, but since his father had been named Old Billy, the nickname had just stuck.

"Oh my god," she stammered, "it's been, like—"

"Long time."

"Yeah." She felt a frantic need to make the conversation smooth, to show that she hadn't changed. "So what's happening?"

"Well, I wish I had better news," he replied, "but let me be direct. Nonna's had a health emergency."

Jessica felt her fingers clutch the edge of her desk. "What is a ... *health emergency*?"

"A stroke."

The world began to spin. Jessica saw her frame of vision narrow. "Is ... is she okay?"

"For now, yes," he said. "They're releasing her from the hospital this afternoon if all her tests go well."

"Is there any *damage*?"

"Her speech is fine," he said, "and her thinking is still pretty straight. The doctor says that mentally she'll be okay. Right now, she's sleeping a lot. The real problem is the work."

"What do you mean?"

"She can't work anymore."

"At all?"

"Doctor said physical labor is out of the question."

Jessica froze. Her grandmother had known this day was coming. She'd talked about it. She was sixty-seven years old, and for nearly fifty of those years had been running her own farm. It wasn't a big operation, only needed three full-time workers, plus some seasonal help, but she'd managed to eke out a decent existence on this earth.

Now it was going to stop.

"So what's the plan?"

"There isn't one," said Young Billy. "She wasn't ready to retire yet. She had plans to work until seventy-five." He sighed. "And we got the summer comin' up."

Jessica felt the anxiety begin in her tailbone, creep up her spine, and out her arms. "Nonna means everything to me."

"I know it," he said. "That's why I called you."

"So what can I do?"

He laughed darkly. "From New York City? I can't think of anything."

"Can I talk to her?"

"Not today. Maybe tomorrow, if she's up for it."

"All right."

"You know we're always thinkin' of you, Jessica. And you're Nonna's favorite anyways."

A rueful smile spread over her face. "I'm going to call you tomorrow."

"You do that."

They disconnected. She sat back. This was like a blow to the forehead. Jessica had spent the most formative years of her life—ages four to six—on that farm. It was her happy place, the place where she indulged in nostalgia. In the bric-a-brac of her memories, it was the one curio that shined the most brightly.

She heard the sound of high heels clicking on the hallway behind their desks. She shivered. That was her boss, Deborah. She was a glamazon, six feet tall, thighs like a body builder. She'd graduated from some impossibly elite university fifteen years earlier, and never stopped talking about it.

"Jessica," she said, without stopping, "there's a meeting upstairs in twenty minutes."

Jessica swiveled in her chair. "We're invited?"

"Don't get excited, it's mandatory. Big announcement."

For a fleeting moment, a worried look appeared on Deborah's face, then it disappeared. Her heels clacked away down the hall.

"See?" said Phineas. "We're moving up already."

Chapter Three

TWENTY MINUTES LATER, the magazine's staff, all forty-three of them, had gathered in the main atrium. Switchbacking up the side wall was a stylishly bare cement staircase. A blue-and-orange abstract expressionist canvas hung from the wall behind it.

Jessica peered up. On the lowest landing of the staircase stood Giovanni Massini, the publisher of *Spretza*. He was a lanky man wearing a dapper Italian suit and crisply gelled hair. Usually Giovanni's attitude vacillated between regular condescension and supreme arrogance, which is why he'd never even noticed Jessica's existence.

This afternoon, however, his face was gray and drawn, and his lips looked tight. Jessica noticed his fingers nervously twisting his rings.

The murmur of the employees fell to a silence as he lifted his hand.

"Gossip goes around the world," he said, "in the time that it takes for truth to get on its shoes. But this time, the gossip is for real. I'm a-going to sell this magazine to another a-company."

Jessica felt all the air suck out of her lungs. The staffers stood there in dumb silence for half a moment. Then they erupted into loud shouts of anger.

Giovanni used his arms to push down the shouts. "Is a good decision," he said, "for a-many reasons. One, I'm a-getting older. Two, advertising is, ah, not the same as it used to be. You know?"

"Who's the buyer?" someone shouted.

"The new owner," said Giovanni, "is New York's most phenomenal magazine company, Grande Cast."

The moans grew louder. Jessica had heard rumors about what a Grande Cast magazine was like to work at. Cold, unforgiving, back-stabbing, penny-pinching—all the characteristics that she'd been taught were wrong from childhood. It was like *Spretza* ratcheted up a hundredfold.

Giovanni continued: "Since eleven years ago, is been my great pleasure to build *Spretza* from the ground. But now is time to find a-new challenge. I sign the paperwork this morning. The new leadership will arrive tomorrow."

There were even more shouts, moans. Slowly it dawned on Jessica why, and then Giovanni spelled it out.

"I cannot guarantee your jobs," he said. "Grande Cast has its own ideas about *Spretza*. My advice is all of you try to learn to fit inside those ideas."

Phineas leaned over. "Translation, we're screwed."

"They'll keep the interns," said Jessica. "Won't they?"

"I don't know about you," said Phineas, "but I'm *way* too fabulous to let go."

All around them, the more senior staffers had already turned away. A few were tapping on their phones, disgusted looks on their faces. Jessica figured that they were already beginning the job search.

"I value the time that we spent together for so many

years," said Giovanni, "and I hope to see all of you somewhere down the road. *Per il futuro.*"

He unsheathed a wicked smile, his white choppers shining brightly in the overhead sodium lighting. There was no applause.

"Good bye," he said, waving again.

A few desultory claps.

Jessica turned away, Phineas with her.

"You can probably forget about that promotion," he said.

"Let's show up tomorrow and see what happens," she said.

Jessica tried to smile, but the tightness in her stomach told a different story.

Chapter Four

IT WAS ONLY their second round of vodka martinis, and Desiree already had her hand down a stranger's pants.

She and Jessica were in a downtown nightclub called Perdition. Going out to the clubs this evening had been Jessica's idea. She'd called Desiree because, of everyone she knew in the city, this tall, mocha-skinned wild child with the springy hair was the only girl who was consistently ready to go out and spend an entire night blowing off stress. Being stressed wasn't even a prerequisite, really. She was ready to go out, anywhere, anytime, period.

Jessica always suspected that Desiree was rebelling against some invisible restriction in her past. It was impossible to get her to open up about her hometown, her family, her history. There was always a change of subject, another glass of champagne, a sudden table dance.

In short, Desiree was a party girl.

That was what Jessica felt that she needed. So she had put on her LBD, or little black dress, which wasn't exactly the most fashion-forward ensemble, but at least it didn't show stains, and was always available in a New York minute. On her feet were some ruby high heels, matching her ruby lipstick. It was a dependable outfit.

No matter what she wore, however, she couldn't command attention quite the way that Desiree did.

Jessica watched the girl on the dance floor, grinding against her hips against the man's hips, her right hand into his front pocket, her left hand making a rodeo lasso motion, her mouth forming a silent *whoop*. Jessica sipped her vodka martini and looked around. The nightclub was two floors of booze, sweat, flesh, lip gloss, loosened ties, stubbly faces, smoky eyes, and loose hands. She wasn't particularly comfortable here, but she really needed to forget about her day, and Perdition was the place to do it.

A man approached Jessica. His collared shirt was professional and his manner was forthright. "What publisher do you work for?" he said.

"I don't."

"You look like you'd be in publishing."

"I'm in magazines."

"That's publishing." He grinned. "You're probably the type of girl who'd rather be at home right now, curled up with a book and a cup of hot chocolate."

Jessica felt piqued. He was halfway right. That was part of herself that she hadn't ever really been able to cover up. "You're totally wrong," she lied. "I'm not like that at all."

"It's okay. I'm into numbers. That's nerdy too."

"Good for you."

"I work at Goldman Sachs."

He waited for that to sink in, but she only shrugged. "You want a pat on the head?"

Resistance. He wasn't used to that. She guessed that he'd dropped the *I work at Goldman Sachs* line plenty of times, that hundreds of other women had begun salivating at the merest mention of his powerful employer. But she'd had quite enough of financial types, thank you.

"This is a good club," he said, changing the subject. "You see the craziest people here."

She shrugged and hid her face behind her glass, wishing he would go away.

"You know," he said, "next time your body wants to have fun, make sure it lets your face know."

"I'm just really stressed right now."

"So am I."

"Maybe we just handle it differently."

He edged in closer. "Listen, you seem like a good girl. But you're in the big city now. And city boys don't like good girls."

Jessica fixed him with a deathly stare. "I've been here for over a year, asshole."

"Then maybe you belong somewhere else," he said.

Smirking, the young financier moved away, down the railing. Jessica watched him open another conversation, with another girl in a little black dress. She could even read his lips. *What publisher do you work for?*

The same canned line.

Jessica shook her head sadly, then wiped the creepy feeling off her arms. Her eyes scanned the dance floor. There was Desiree, ripping off her shirt now, nothing left on top but a brassiere. Several men had circled to watch the striptease.

She lowered her head. Jessica had known things would end up this way. Tonight, she was the one who needed to act out, to unwind, but she couldn't. Meanwhile, Desiree always ignored the circumstances and stole the show no matter where she was, or what her role. It served Jessica right, though, for hanging out with New York's biggest attention whore.

Jessica would have to act like designated friend tonight, keeping the wild girl out of trouble. She gulped the rest of her vodka martini, set down the glass, and threaded her way onto the dance floor.

The bodies were packed tightly, and the moist animal heat of engorged flesh filled Jessica's nostrils. She slid her way through the throng, feeling a line of perspiration springing out on her upper lip. At last she came upon Desiree.

"You're having a good time," said Jessica.

"For *real*," Desiree replied. Her eyes were shut, her head thrown backwards—and a man's hands were groping her bra.

"I need to go to the bathroom," said Jessica.

Desiree opened her eyes and looked down on Jessica. "Right now?"

"Right now."

Desiree tried to disengage herself from her male admirer, but his hands seemed to have been made of Velcro. She finally pulled them off.

Holding hands, Jessica dragged Desiree through the crowded dance floor. In the space of one minute, no less than eight men tried to either talk to, dance with, or simply grab Desiree. Jessica gripped the girl's hand even more tightly and pulled her into the bathroom.

Here, the music was a distant throbbing, and the voices could be heard. At the sink, Jessica turned to her friend.

"I don't want to sound like I'm complaining," she said, "but I asked you to come hang out with me."

"Well, you ain't dancin'," answered Desiree, "and I don't like standing outside. I like to be where the action is."

"The action seems happening inside your bra."

"Get me another drink and we'll hang out," she said, reapplying lipstick in the mirror.

"I'm not going to get you a drink. You've got ATMs all over this club ready to get you drinks." Jessica tugged on her arm. It was warm to the touch and slick with sweat. "Look, I need your attention right now."

The girl's brown eyes slid sideways. "Girl, you've *got* to chill."

Jessica felt the tightness in her stomach returning. "You don't know what's happening to my job. I need someone to *help* me."

Desiree twisted the lipstick closed. "I can help you on the dance floor. Come on." This time, she took Jessica by the hand, and led her out of the bathroom back towards the dance floor.

———

Two hours later, Jessica burst back into the bathroom. She'd had four vodka martinis and was barely upright.

But Desiree was worse. She'd accepted every drink, puff, line, stimulant, depressant, upper, and downer that had been offered to her. Now Jessica was literally holding the girl up, her right arm hooked under both of Desiree's armpits, dragging her towards one of the toilets.

Inside the dirty stall, Desiree collapsed to her knees and clutched the sides of the white bowl. The vomit came fast and colorful. Jessica stood behind her, holding the girl's hair back. She wondered how the night could've gone so wrong. She hadn't wanted to play den mother.

When Desiree was finished, her head dropped down to the toilet. Her forehead rested on the rim. Jessica flinched at the filth that must be crawling onto her face.

"Come on, girl," she said. "Let's get a taxi."

No response. She shook Desiree's shoulder. "Come on, stand up. We'll get you some water."

Slowly, Desiree's body slumped to the left, her torso wedging itself between the toilet and the wall. An open eyelid showed that her eyeball had rolled upwards in its socket.

Jessica shrieked. This wasn't any ordinary night out. This

had morphed into something much worse. She squeezed the girl's face between her fingers, slapped her cheeks lightly, hoping to wake her up. "Come *on*, Desiree, wake up, *don't* do this, *please* don't—"

No response. Jessica chewed on a knuckle. She couldn't carry the girl out of here, since Desiree was five foot ten, probably a hundred and sixty pounds. Jessica was half a foot shorter and petite.

The only other alterative was to call an ambulance. That would cost money, paperwork, you name it.

Jessica was trying to think of another course of action when Desiree's body suddenly began to violently shake. Those weren't twitches.

They were full-on convulsions.

Jessica booted open the door to the stall. A small group of girls had noticed the commotion inside and were circled around. Their mouths were little open circles of panic.

"Call security," said Jessica, "*right now*."

Chapter Five

THE NEXT MORNING AT WORK, Jessica sat on her stool, staring emptily at the garbage barge, feeling a bit dazed.

She turned and looked instead at the picture on her desk. It was of herself, age six, and her grandmother, Nonna. They were holding a little piglet together. Jessica was wearing gingham overalls and her hair had been twisted into pigtails. As a teenager, Jessica had seen that photo as a reference to her own pigginess, since she'd been thirty pounds overweight. Over three years, in fact, she'd tried every fad diet in the world. Nothing had worked. In college, she'd even started throwing up.

Eventually she'd wrestled her way down to this acceptable weight. She still didn't have much muscular definition, but at least in silhouette Jessica was shaped like a normal woman. She was nobody's first choice, never would be, but she comforted herself with the fact that she wouldn't be anybody's consolation prize either.

Phineas noticed her silence. "Your grandma is sexy," he said, nodding at the picture.

"Don't be gross."

"No, I'm serious. She looks sure of herself. It's attractive."

"Nonna has worked on a farm her whole life."

"That's probably why she's sure of herself."

It made sense. Jessica pondered that for a minute. Then she sighed. "That's my Nonna."

"The one who raised you."

"Only for a few years."

"But they were the important ones."

"Yes."

Phineas passed her an Advil and a cup of coffee. "Don't start talking about Mom and Dad again. I've exceeded my monthly limit of pathos."

Jessica winced. She knew what he was referring to. Last month, they'd spent five hours drinking red wine while she related the story of her dysfunctional parents.

"Oh, come on. Let's see if you remember."

"I was drunk that night," said Phineas, "and it was totally your fault."

"Just try."

He thought back, finger on chin. "Short story was, your dad skipped town, and your mom's a codependent failure."

Jessica nodded. "That about sums it up. Would you like to hear my newest story?"

Phineas waved a hand. "No, the couch is closed. The doctor is out."

"My friend Desiree had to go to the hospital last night."

"Let me guess. Public health officials found a massive crab infestation in her vagina."

"No," said Jessica, "it was alcohol poisoning. They measured her blood level at point seventeen."

Phineas slapped his hand on his desk. "That does it. I'm officially turning her into a character in my newest comic series."

Jessica stared at her thumb. "I don't know why I'm friends with her."

"Because she doesn't judge."

"Maybe."

"Unlike me. I'm a nasty old queen."

"Shut up."

Jessica opened another box. It was a yellow vinyl pump with a bizarre curlicued strap. "I don't even know *how* I would wear this," she said.

Then her phone rang. She looked at the caller ID. It was Desiree.

Jessica quickly picked up. "Are you okay? I stayed with you in the room until five in the morning."

The girl's voice was tiny and haggard. "No, I'm not okay."

"Are you still at the hospital?"

"No, they discharged me two hours ago. I'm back in my apartment." She paused, then said, "My mom is here."

That was odd. Desiree never mentioned her family. "So what does that mean?"

"She's taking me away."

"To where."

"Home."

"But aren't you at home?"

"No, she's taking me to her home. In North Carolina."

Jessica nearly dropped the phone. "Why?"

"She says the city is ruining me."

Jessica couldn't think of anything to say to that. It was hard to disagree. "She really should've talked it over with you—"

Desiree interrupted. "Listen, she said she'd cut me off. No phone, no rent money, nothing. I can't afford to live here."

"Your mom pays your rent?"

"Of course. I can't afford this damn city on my own."

Jessica thought how she was doing exactly that: paying her own way.

Try as she might, there wasn't much else to say. "I'm totally floored," she admitted.

"So my mom wants to say something to you," said Desiree.

"To me?"

"Yeah. Hold on, here she is."

There were the muffled sounds of the phone being handed over, and a stern woman's voice came online. "Is this Jessica?"

"Yes."

"I'm Helen. I don't appreciate the way you have corrupted my daughter."

"Excuse me?"

"She was an absolutely perfect *angel* until you laid your filthy hands on her."

Jessica felt her heart erupt out of her chest. "You seem to have misunderstood—"

"No, I understand perfectly. Mary Jean was a pious girl very active in our church until she convinced me to move to this godforsaken city—"

Jessica sat up. "*Mary Jean*? Who is *Mary Jean*?"

"—and now she's become the whore of Babylon. And she says that *you're* to blame."

"That is absolute *bullshit*—"

"The cursing isn't helping your cause, young lady. I would advise you find Jesus, quick. And don't try to contact my daughter."

The call ended. Jessica looked at her phone, in absolute shock. Then she mouthed a curse word to herself. Her so-called friend, Desiree, or whatever she was calling herself, hadn't been mature enough to take responsibility for her own actions. She'd pointed a finger straight at Jessica instead.

"People suck," said Jessica, to nobody in particular.

"Then this is probably the wrong time to tell you that Deborah stopped by your desk at eight o'clock am."

Jessica looked at him. "Why would she do that? Nobody gets here until at least nine am."

"I don't know. But she came by again at eight-thirty. She wanted to know when you'd be here."

That was bad news.

Then, behind her, Jessica heard a click-clacking on the floor. A moment later, the voice of her glamazon boss sounded sharp and tight.

"Jessica, can I talk to you for a minute, please?"

Chapter Six

HER HEART POUNDING in her chest, Jessica swiveled around on her stool. "Right now?"

"Yes, now."

"Okay."

Jessica stood up. Deborah crooked a finger and Jessica found herself falling in line behind her. She turned back and looked at Phineas. He'd lifted a small flag from his pencil jar and was waving it back and forth.

Deborah led her towards the women's restroom. She opened the door.

"In here?" said Jessica.

"Yes."

It was a single small room, nothing but a toilet, a sink, a mirror, and a chair. It wasn't the type of place they normally held conferences.

Jessica stepped inside. Deborah closed the door behind them and locked it. She sat down on the chair. "Please, have a seat."

She was gesturing towards the toilet.

"Really?" said Jessica.

"You're going to want to be sitting down," replied Deborah, "and this chair is mine."

Jessica looked at the toilet. "But there's no lid."

"Just sit."

Jessica sat down quickly on the toilet. This was the most embarrassing meeting she'd ever endured.

"So," said Deborah.

"This sounds serious."

Deborah took a deep breath. "Grande Mast is bringing in their own people this week."

"We already know that."

"Stuff a sock in it and *listen*. I thought you would like to know that they're *also* bringing in the Grande Mast internship program."

Jessica felt herself sinking into the toilet. Her heels were angled inwards a little. "What does that mean?"

"It means you're going to be made redundant."

Jessica tilted her head. "I don't understand."

"That's British for *they don't need you anymore*."

"So I'm fired?"

"It's a little different. You'll just become unnecessary. Unless you can convince Grande Mast to accept you into their internship program."

"I'll do that, then."

"It's incredibly competitive," said Deborah.

"How competitive?"

"Last year, they rejected three girls who'd graduated from the Sorbonne."

"What's that?"

Deborah smiled condescendingly. "Don't worry about it. Listen, girls your age are constitutionally unable to take good advice, but I'll give it anyways." She paused. "You should leave the magazine."

"Why?"

"Because it'll be easier than getting ignored, fired, whatever by the new overlords. And this way you'll keep your dignity."

Jessica thought about that. She was probably right.

"But what about you?"

Deborah smoothed her hair in the mirror. "Oh, don't worry about me. I'm a survivor."

"I mean, could you put in a good word for me?"

Deborah turned and gave her a pitiful half-smile, the type you give to a poor, wounded animal that's not going to last the night. "I'll give you a good reference, Jessica. You have my word on that."

On the toilet, Jessica suddenly felt sick and hunched over. She could feel her rear end slipping down into the bowl. Suddenly Deborah reached over and pushed the flush handle. The water below her ass convulsed.

Jessica yelped and leapt off the toilet. "What the hell?"

"This," said Deborah, "is a wakeup call. It's time to shit or get off the pot."

"*Jesus—*"

"Now, I'm going to ask you a question."

"Okay."

Deborah crossed her arms. "Do you really want to work in fashion?"

"Of course. I love fashion."

"But do you *need* it?"

Jessica thought about the words *want* and *need*. "What's the difference?"

Deborah stood up. She was a full head taller than Jessica. "Could you live any other way?"

Jessica's eyes shifted sideways. Dandling one foot behind the other, she thought about the photo on her desk, of Nonna and the piglet on the farm.

"Yeah, I guess I *could*. But I'd rather—"

Deborah looked at her young intern, her lips pursed, but her eyes brimming with sympathy.

"Then you don't *need* it," she said.

Jessica didn't say anything. There were too many thoughts flying through her head. "This is ... a lot."

Deborah brushed off her coat, then went to the sink and washed her hands. Jessica realized that she'd never used the chair. "Well, don't take too long thinking in here. Other people need to use the toilet too."

Her boss dried her hands, smiled professionally, and left the bathroom. Jessica stood, leaning against the wall, stunned.

A moment later, there was a knock on the door.

"It's occupied," she said.

Phineas popped his head inside. "I bet that was totally hot. The two of you should be totally ashamed."

"Shut up."

"If I were straight, I'd be really turned on right now."

"Phineas," she said, "Deborah just told me to leave the magazine."

He looked crestfallen. Then a sly grin spread over his face.

"So you got canned ... in the can."

Jessica slugged him in the shoulder.

"I am *not* in the mood for jokes."

"How can I make it up to you?"

She stared at him. "You can help me pack up my desk."

Chapter Seven

THAT AFTERNOON, Jessica lay on her back, staring at the blue sky, feeling the cool wind whip across her bare arms and legs, the crisp blades of green grass poking into her back. It felt like a tiny massage from the earth. A reassurance from the dirt that life would, in fact, continue.

She was laying in Sheep's Meadow in Central Park. There were a hundred or so other sunbathers spread out across the vast lawn, picnickers, families, professionals, drifters—all drawn to this city by vague dreams of urban success.

And some were at a loss about how to achieve any it.

Jessica looked up at the clouds. She saw a horse, galloping across the sky. Then she watched as they reformed into a cow. Next came a pig.

She rubbed her eyes. The universe was giving her a sign.

Jessica needed to leave the city.

Practically speaking, she couldn't afford to stay in the city any longer anyways. Two thousand dollars a month for a tiny closet in Brooklyn, fifteen dollars minimum for a take-out lunch. Without a steady paycheck, it wasn't feasible.

Emotionally, she could feel herself checking out too. Her

whole life here, practically, had been bound up in *Spretza*. She'd enjoyed nothing except work, wine, sleep, wake up. Rinse and repeat.

It would take at least four months to find another internship, or job, that was as remotely promising. That was really the only reason to live in New York for an outsider. There was no sense in staying if she was content with an ordinary job. The cost of living was too high. If she wanted to open a cupcake shop, for instance, there were plenty of more practical places to do so than in the center of modern financial life.

Suddenly, she felt the world differently. Jessica began to see past the skyscrapers of Manhattan that towered around all four areas of this park, past the ugly heels, past her own ambitions.

She began to see what really mattered.

Jessica pulled out her phone. She opened her contacts list. Her finger dialed Nonna's number.

Young Billy answered.

"Hello," he said.

"It's Jessica," she replied. "I'm coming back to the farm."

Chapter Eight

JESSICA STEPPED to the curb at the small airport, dragging a pair of heavy duffle bags and a fabric suitcase. She smelled the air.

It smelled rich and humid. Like home.

A white Ford F150 was approaching her. It was spattered with mud around the bottom edges and sported mud flaps behind the rear wheels. Jessica cocked her head. She hadn't seen a vehicle like this in a long time.

It pulled to a stop. The driver's door opened, and a tall, gangly man stepped out. He was wearing a simple plaid shirt, jeans, and a pair of well-worn work boots. His face was broad and his high cheekbones looked sharp enough to open cans. His face said trustworthy.

"Young Billy," she said. "It is *so good* to see you."

"Likewise, kiddo." Young Billy wrapped his long arms around her and gave her a long squeeze. It felt better and lasted longer than any hug she had ever received in the city. "Nonna is real excited to see you. That's all she's talked about for the last two weeks."

He bent down, lifted her bags, and easily tossed them into the bed of the truck.

"There is some breakable stuff in there," she said.

"Sorry, darling," said Young Billy. "The pigs aren't quite as sensitive."

She climbed into the passenger seat of the cab. It was clean. In the dashboard was a satellite radio.

Young Billy eased the car out of the pickup zone and onto the freeway. When they'd left the airport far behind, he finally exhaled. "Congestion makes me get all worked up. I need my elbow room. Coffee?"

He gestured to the cup holder, where a paper cup was waiting.

"For me?"

"Of course. I brewed it this morning."

Jessica smelled it. "Drip coffee?"

"Oh. Let me guess. You probably like espresso now."

Young Billy was right—there had been a mandatory cappuccino break every morning at *Spretza*—but Jessica decided it was better not to admit that. She replaced the paper cup back in the holder. "I'm okay for now."

Young Billy reached forward to the satellite radio. "It's goin' to be a long drive, and I'm not much for talkin', so we'd better put some music on."

He hit the power button, and the sounds of lap-steel guitar exploded out of the speakers. He immediately turned it down. "Sorry. I like it kinda loud when I'm by myself."

She listened to the music for a while. In perfectly clear enunciation, the singer was complaining that he couldn't ever get drunk enough to forget his problems. Jessica hadn't heard any music like this in a long time. In New York City, she'd only listened to Dutch electronic beats, which were challenging. This music, though, was neither. It was exactly what you expected, exactly what you wanted.

"What do you think?" said Young Billy.

"Of what?"

"The music."

"It's not my favorite."

"This is Blake Shelton. He's my favorite. He's got a really good voice."

She shrugged. "It's okay, I guess."

"Stay out here for a while, and you'll come to like it."

The truck rolled off the highway, turned west, and headed out into the rolling fields. Jessica's stomach rose and fell as the vehicle floated up and down the gentle crests and troughs.

Young Billy rolled down the windows. "Let's get some fresh air in here. You probably haven't smelled this in a while."

Jessica inhaled deeply. The smell of clover, of pine, of earth filled her nostrils. It was alluring.

"That smells great," she said.

"You can't get tired of it," said Young Billy. "So, there's something I should probably tell you about."

"What's that?"

"There've been some changes at the farm recently. We sold the Holsteins."

She nodded. "Nonna told me last year."

"No more dairy. The new regulations were impossible. We just got out completely. It's easier this way."

For a moment, Jessica lost herself in nostalgia. During her two years on the farm, she'd been assigned the job of milking the family's three dairy cows. It'd been strange at first, squatting on the stool, squeezing the teats, but she'd quickly grown used to it. Of course there'd been plenty of modern equipment that could have done the task, but with only three cows, Nonna had said it was unnecessary. Mostly, she hadn't wanted to invest in the machinery, not when your granddaughter would do it for free. In New York, Jessica had noticed that people tended to stare, then burst into laughter, when she admitted to knowing how to milk a cow, so eventually she'd stopped talking about it.

Soon the land flattened out, and Jessica felt a stab in her heart as she recognized the local general store.

Hackmore's.

It'd been done up like a big red barn, even though it was a normal concrete structure underneath. She was glad to see that it had stayed the same. The big sliding front doors were still in place. The bales of hay out front. It still even had the adorably hick sign, a man in overalls with a hayseed in his teeth.

"Good to see some things don't change," she said.

"That's not exactly true," said Young Billy. "Hackmore's goin' through some rough times. The old man died last year, and his kid doesn't want to keep it open."

"Why?"

"The corporate farms don't buy so much as a single seed there. They got their own distributor for everything." He shook his head. "Hackmore's is antiquated. It's from another time."

"I remember playing on the sacks inside when I was little."

Young Billy smiled. "I played on those sacks too. Don't get me wrong, we buy from them when we can, because I'd hate to see them close. Jesus, I'd have to drive sixty-five extra miles, one way, just to get a few extra bags of feed."

A few miles later, the plains were broken by a stand of trees that ran parallel with the road. Alongside the trees, about thirty meters in, was a creek.

Jessica craned her head. "The creek hasn't changed either. Still tiny."

"When those thunderstorms roll through," he said, "you better stay the hell away from that creek."

"I remember," she said.

He suddenly grew serious. "No, it's *worse* than you remember."

"What do you mean?"

"I don't know why the weather has changed, but everything's real screwy now. Every year for the last six years, that creek floods higher and more often than before. Last year it ruined Kilkenny's soy crop."

Jessica remembered how Kilkenny's property was at least a hundred meters away from the creek. "That's pretty scary," she said.

He nodded. "You'd better believe it. Personally, though, I think it would take an act of God for flood waters to touch Nonna's toes. And if they tried, she'd probably point her finger and tell that dirty water to jump right back to wherever it came from."

Jessica laughed. Feared but respected, her grandmother was not a personality to be taken lightly.

As Young Billy slowed the truck, Jessica felt her heartbeat speed up. There, on the right, was the familiar long deer fence —actually two fences, about a foot apart, to discourage jumping.

Then the driveway appeared. The simple sign hadn't changed: *Nonna's Farms.*

Jessica felt the warmth spread like syrup through her body, first in her thighs, then up into her chest and down into her feet. If there was any place on earth that needed to stay the same, this was it. And Nonna was making sure of that.

Young Billy cranked the wheel of the truck, and they rumbled down the dirt road, the bare springtime fields on either side, towards a distant structure.

Nonna's house.

Chapter Nine

AS THE FARMHOUSE grew larger in the windshield, Jessica held her breath, hoping that nothing had changed.

Her wish was granted. Nonna's house still had the same white eaves, the same freshly painted red plank walls. The same lace curtains in the kitchen windows. The same octagonal attic window through which Jessica, as a child, had peered during rainstorms.

"Thank God," said Jessica.

"Nonna knows how she likes things to look," Young Billy said. "And she keeps a tight ship."

They pulled up underneath a large elm. To the west of the farmhouse, a tall line of fourteen closely-spaced Italian cypress acted as a windbreak.

Jessica stepped out of the truck. There was a distinct chill in the air, and she pulled her coat more tightly around her.

Young Billy hauled her bags out of the back. "I'll take these inside and let Nonna know that you're here."

"Can I come inside?"

He paused, thinking. "I have to see how she's doing today. Hold on."

He disappeared into the house carrying her bags, one in each hand, as if each were no heavier than a loaf of bread. Jessica watched him. That was the easy strength that a lifetime of hard, outdoor work gives a person.

In the meantime, Jessica strolled around the property, hands in pockets, feeling sweetly nostalgic. She paused to look at the old wooden tool shed, its paint long since worn off by the harsh winters. It was nearing sixty years of age. It would be easy to order a manufactured metal replacement from any number of farm catalogs, she guessed, but Nonna probably didn't see any point, especially if it cost money.

She passed around the back of the house, then stopped. There was the small wooden tub that Nonna used to bathe her in. Inside the house was a shower, of course, but young Jessica had insisted that she soap up outdoors. Now she remembered how her grandmother had humored her, shampooing her hair, dipping a pitcher into the tub and pouring the warm water onto her small head.

It was her favorite memory from childhood.

And out beyond the tub were the fields. Jessica turned and surveyed them, drinking in the landscape, the empty brown furrows, the long aluminum sprinklers waiting patiently for the fallow fields to be replanted.

"They told me you'd be coming back, Jessie," said a man's voice.

Jessica whirled around. It was a small, thin man wearing a work shirt, denim pants, and a pair of oversized boots. A length of rope was wound around his right shoulder. On his head was an enormous cowboy hat; on his face was a sneer.

This was Stanley, the farm manager. Until now, Jessica had avoided thinking about him. He'd been hired by Nonna a few years earlier for his technological knowledge, and since then, he'd slowly been pulling Nonna into the twenty-first century. That was his best characteristic, and his only good one.

"My name's Jessica," she said, "and yes, I'm back."

Stanley smirked. "There must've been a sudden mascara shortage for you to flee the city."

"Funny," she replied, "but I did grow up here, you know."

"For two years."

She ignored that. "I notice you're still wearing the hat."

"Why not?"

"Why don't you just wear a baseball cap like everybody else?"

"Because I'm country as hell, and always will be—that's why." He spat on the ground for emphasis.

"Listen," she said, "we have to get along. For Nonna's sake."

"Aw, to hell with Nonna," he said. "She wouldn't know a smartphone app if it bit her in the ass."

"She's almost seventy years old," said Jessica, getting upset, "and please watch your tone. She's my *grandmother*."

"You haven't been here," he answered. "You haven't seen how stubborn and backwards that woman can be. If it were up to her, we'd still be breaking the ground with a spade while hollerin' field songs to one another."

Jessica sniffed. "Whatever."

"There's the city girl attitude," he said, poking a finger at her. "I knew it wouldn't be long. Oh, that's gonna fly real well. For sure."

"We're getting off on the wrong foot."

He stepped forward, hands on hips, getting close into her face. "First, you have to prove yourself."

"I don't have to prove anything," she said.

"Nonna Farms can't afford any dead weight. We're a bare-bones operation already."

"So?"

"So you have to contribute."

"I will."

41

Stanley smirked. "Don't be so sure of that. Things have changed. And you've changed too. Or so they tell me."

"Who tells you?"

He shook his head, ignoring the question. "I'll see you at supper. Make us something good."

"I'm cooking?"

"Well, Nonna sure as hell ain't. She can barely stand. And you're the only other woman."

Jessica felt the city girl in herself bristle at the insinuation. But before she could respond, Young Billy stepped out outside. "Jessica," he said, "she's ready to talk. Better make it fast before she conks out again."

Chapter Ten

THE FARMHOUSE HADN'T CHANGED a whit.

Jessica stepped through the front door. The living room was as sunny and as tidy as ever. The orange-and-green afghan was laid neatly over the back of the faded couch. Motes of dust floated lazily through the air.

Jessica kicked off her boots. The wooden floorboards felt warm beneath her feet. They'd always felt warm, no matter what the season. There was no explanation for it. It was nearly magical.

Young Billy poured himself a glass of water at a tank with a spigot. "Your bags are in the spare bedroom."

"What about the attic?" said Jessica. "That's where I always used to stay."

"There's a leak in the roof."

"I don't care."

He looked at her as though she had just suggested sleeping on a dried cow patty. "If it rains, you'll be in trouble."

"We keep an eye on the weather," she replied. "Can you move my stuff there?"

"Are you sure?"

"Yeah."

He finished his water, then went off to move the bags.

In the meantime, Jessica tentatively poked her head in the kitchen. The sight of it made her heart warm. It had barreled straight out of the nineteen fifties. A small Frigidaire icebox stood along one wall. An old stove with heavy black prongs occupied the space beneath a heavy hood.

"All right," said Young Billy, "come on back."

She moved quickly down the small hallway, towards the door at the end, which stood halfway open.

Nonna's room.

As Jessica walked down the hallway, she felt the years rolling backwards, the worries and disappointments flaking away. She remembered feeling like this almost twenty years ago. This is how the world felt as a child.

Then she saw Nonna, and that fantasy disappeared.

In her queen bed, propped halfway up on a pile of pillows, was her grandmother. She wore a lace nightgown that went nearly to her neck. Her hair had been wrapped into a bun, affixed with several black pins. Nonna had never cut her hair, not once in nearly half a century of farm labor. That and the mahogany sleigh bed frame were her only concessions to luxury.

But her face had changed. The left half of Nonna's proud countenance was drooping slightly downwards.

"Jessie," she said, slightly slurring.

"*Nonna.*"

Jessica rushed across the bedroom and flung her arms around her grandmother. While she'd been stronger than most men, Nonna now felt weak. It was an odd sensation.

Her grandmother disengaged and looked away, out the window, her left hand covering her eyes. Jessica realized that she was crying.

"It's an embarrassment to be seen like this," said the old woman.

"No, it's not."

"This wasn't meant to happen. At least, not yet."

"We don't get to choose these things."

Nonna looked at her oddly. "Dammit, why do you have to make *sense*? You're absolutely *nothing* like your mother."

Jessica pulled up a chair along her bedside. "Well, somebody had to be the grownup."

"Are you two talking?"

Jessica shook her head. "Dennis won't let her."

"Not even to you?"

"No."

Nonna shook her head sadly. Then she cleared it out of her head. Jessica knew that Nonna had made peace with her daughter's poor choices years earlier, and had simply looked past her to the next generation.

To Jessica.

"So New York City couldn't hold onto you," said Nonna.

"No, I couldn't hold onto *it*."

"It seems like an interesting place. Always something happening."

Something about Nonna's manner led her to believe that her grandmother was, for one moment, rethinking her choices in life, imagining different roads.

"What do you think of my new face?"

"You don't look too bad."

Nonna looked pensive. "It may or may not recover, but I'm not worried about that. If it doesn't, I'll fit right in with the horses."

Jessica laughed in spite of herself. "They certainly don't care."

"Here's the real problem. Look at my left arm."

Jessica helped her roll down the bedsheet and uncovered

her grandmother's arm. She nearly gasped. It was totally immobile, the hand hooked like a frozen little claw.

"Strokes," she said, "apparently affect different people in different ways. My face got off easy compared with this poor arm."

"But nothing mental?"

Her grandmother grinned. "Just the same problem I've always had. Stubborn as a mule."

Jessica smiled. "Are you going to go to therapy?"

Nonna nodded. "The doctor calls it constrained-use therapy. Basically they tie down my left arm and make me use the right one. I start tomorrow. Young Billy has to drive me."

"Maybe Stanley can help."

The old woman rolled her eyes. "No thank you. I couldn't sit in a car with him for more than five minutes without hearing about all those newest gadgets and doohickeys."

"Well, I'm here to help," said Jessica proudly.

"So you are, Jessie. So you are."

Nonna was studying her, a detached expression on her face.

"What?" said Jessica.

Nonna took her hand. "We're at the edge of the cliff, financially."

"You don't have to pay me," she replied.

"I appreciate that, but I'm depending on you to do everything that I used to."

Jessica nodded. "I won't let you down."

"You pick up some city ways?"

"A few," said Jessica, "but they're already gone. I threw them in the trash before I boarded the airplane."

Nonna arched an eyebrow. "Is that so?"

Jessica nodded. "I promise."

"All right, if you say so. You are now a full working member of this farm. Young Billy will go over your list of duties later. Right now, your first assignment is due at five-thirty."

Jessica felt her stomach drop. She knew what was coming. "What's that?"

"You need to make dinner."

"For everybody?"

"Yes. These three men can't boil a hot dog. And I won't let them eat any of that microwaved frozen crap. They need real food. Homemade."

"I'm on it," she said.

Nonna nodded. "You should probably get started ... let me show you..."

Her grandmother's eyes grew unfocused. Her mouth fell open. Jessica waited for further instructions, but the only thing that escaped the old woman's mouth was a snore.

As she stared at her suddenly unconscious grandmother, Jessica realized that she was on her own.

Chapter Eleven

IN THE KITCHEN, Jessica flung open the pantry and took a quick inventory.

It hadn't been too difficult to come up with ideas. In the refrigerator she'd found a bag of ripe tomatoes and a container of goat cheese. There was some olive oil and vinegar in a cupboard. Add some basil, and that would make a delicious Caprese salad. She'd developed a taste for them in New York. It was the perfect food for health.

But that was just an appetizer. The men needed protein too. Jessica raided the freezer and found four whole trout, each about a third of a pound. She could douse them in olive oil, sprinkle some spices, then bake quickly.

They still needed carbohydrates. Ransacking the cupboards, she spotted the dependable orange box. Uncle Ben's rice. There was about a cup and a half left. That would probably be enough.

It was a tasteful, healthy dinner. But she only had forty minutes to make it. In a kitchen she hadn't used in years.

She hadn't cooked anything while in New York either. It hadn't been out of laziness. The kitchen in her tiny apartment had consisted of a mini-refrigerator, a stove with two mini-burners, an oven that couldn't bake anything bigger than a potato, and a countertop the size of a placemat.

She'd eaten all of her meals outside the home—at cafeterias, restaurants, bars, on the street. She'd traded tips with other interns about the best hot dog vendors. She'd stolen food from luncheon buffets in the conference room.

In the meantime, her cooking skills had shrunken to the size of a nickel.

Jessica tied an apron around her waist, realized it was backwards, then retied it. Hands trembling, she set a pot of water on the stove, then began clearing a space on the kitchen counter for the fish. She soaked it in hot water, then began to cut off the heads. On her first try, the knife slipped in her hands, nearly severing a thumb.

When the water was boiling, she poured the rice in, tossed some salt into the water, then covered with the lid. That finished, she began preheating the oven. She carefully lined a baking sheet with aluminum foil, covered it generously in olive oil, then swabbed the fish in the stuff. She squeezed lemon over the package, sprinkled salt and pepper, then shook some dill out of an ancient shaker.

The oven felt hot enough, so she opened the door, slid the fish onto the rack, and shut the door. Then she turned to the cutting board. It had fish juice on it. She needed to wash it before using it again. Jessica was proud that she had remembered.

She began slicing the tomatoes, arranging the slices onto four plates. She alternated each tomato slice with a dollop of goat cheese. It would've been more authentic with mozzarella, or even better, burrata, but this would have to do. At last, she finished a red-and-white striped circle of yumminess on each plate. She sprinkled salt and pepper on each, then drizzled olive oil and balsamic vinegar.

Basil. She'd forgotten to ask about that.

Jessica left the kitchen and ran outside the house. Stanley was carrying a stack of brown plastic trays with egg-shaped slots into the greenhouse. He staggered a little beneath the tower of plastic.

"Stanley," she said, "do we have any basil?"

He turned his head. "We stopped growing herbs six years ago, Jessie."

"It's *Jessica*. And I mean, are there any in the house?"

He frowned. "What are you making with basil?"

"You'll see."

"I really don't know."

Jessica shrugged. She'd just leave the Caprese salad the way it was.

As she turned the corner, the acrid smell of burning food reached her nostrils. It wasn't hard to find the culprit. It was the rice. She ran over to the stove and lifted the lid. It was pure iron and seared her fingers. Yelping, she dropped the lid onto the floor.

She went to the sink, ran her fingers under the water, wrapped them in a paper towel, then went back to the stove. The burner was set on high. That was a problem. She'd forgotten to lower to a simmer, and now the rice had burned itself into a hard crust around the edges of the pot. All that was left was a small bowlful of white rice in the middle, a cupful at most.

At that moment, the front door slammed. The heavy sounds of boots on floorboards, the sound of raucous laughter. That was Young Billy and Stanley. Then she heard a third man cough. That was the seasonal worker. Young Billy said he'd just arrived a couple of days ago.

"Dinner's almost ready," she shouted.

"I am starved," said Young Billy.

"Hope you like basil," said Stanley.

"What?"

In the kitchen, Ainsley scraped the usable rice out of the pot and divvied it up onto four separate plates. There was only about three spoonfuls left per person. Then she opened the oven and withdrew the baking sheet. She'd overbaked the fish too. They looked like four hard, dry fish-paddles.

She was resolved to make the best of it. The men had already sat down at the farmhouse-style table, a long bench on each side. The third man, a Mexican, sat quietly in a long-sleeved t-shirt, blue jeans, and work boots. He glanced at Jessica quickly, then glanced away.

"I already got the napkins and silverware," said Young Billy.

"Thank you," she said.

"This is Ernesto," he said. "He doesn't speak English. *Habla espanol solamente.*"

"Nice to meet you," said Jessica.

The seasonal worker smiled, then dropped his gaze to his lap.

She rounded the table and delivered the Caprese salad to each man. They looked down at their plates, mystified.

"What is this?" said Stanley. "A vegetable candy cane?"

"Italians eat this all the time," answered Jessica. "It's called a Caprese salad."

"We're not in Italy."

"Just try it."

Young Billy chewed for a moment. "It's good. I'd order that in a restaurant."

Stanley tasted it. "Could use basil, though."

Ignoring him, Jessica went back to the kitchen and brought out the fish and rice.

"I like fish sometimes," said Young Billy.

"But not sushi," said Stanley.

"No, the Japanese can keep that stuff. But this looks good. Baked, right?"

Stanley studied his plate, then shrugged and tucked into his food. Ernesto and Young Billy had already started.

"That needs some liquid," said Stanley.

Jessica began to cut her fish. "Be kind," she said, "it's my first attempt."

"We don't get this kind of treatment everyday," said Young Billy. "A multi-course extravaganza."

"What's next?" replied Stanley.

She felt their eyes upon her. Jessica looked up, her fork frozen in midair.

Young Billy was looking at her expectantly. Stanley was smirking. Ernesto was waiting. All three plates had been scraped clean.

"You guys are finished already?" she said.

"We were hungry," said Young Billy.

"You were *really* hungry."

"We still are," said Stanley.

Jessica set down her fork, rubbed the heels of her palms into her eye sockets. Then she said, "That's everything."

The men were quiet.

Then Stanley said, "Jessica, this is a working farm."

"I know."

"And real men at a real working farm develop real appetites."

"I'm sorry."

Stanley ran his finger around the olive oil on his plate, then flicked it backwards over his shoulder. "This stuff may be stylish in New York, but it's not really our kind of fuel. We need butter, carbs, bacon."

"But Nonna—"

"Nonna what? Wasn't awake to help you?"

"Yes."

Stanley shook his head. "Do you know how many times we could've used her help in the last few weeks? I've been here seven years, and there's *still* things I don't know about this property."

Jessica felt a mixture of anger and self-disgust. "So what are you saying?"

"Stop complaining and start learning."

The challenge hung there between them like a drop of blood dangling from the end of a needle.

Then Stanley wiped his mouth and stood up. "Fellas, there's a McDonald's in town. My treat."

Young Billy stood. "Sorry, Jessica. You'll get the hang of this."

She watched the three men stand up and leave the house. She heard the doors of Young Billy's truck open, then close. She listened to the truck drive off.

Then, sitting alone at the long wooden table, hearing nothing but the cold spring wind whistling against the eaves of the farmhouse, her stylish, small dinner cooling on her plate—

Jessica began to realize that the city might've changed her more than she'd thought.

Chapter Twelve

"THIS EARTH," said Stanley, "is our lifeblood. It's what pays our bills. Don't mess it up."

It was sunrise the next morning, and Jessica was looking out over Nonna's property. She was wearing a sweatshirt under a blue jean jacket, an old pair of work jeans, and a new pair of boots. On her head was a plaid hunter's cap with the earflaps pulled down. It was Nonna's cap, forty years of her sweat sunk into the brow. In the city, it would be worn ironically by a skinny-jeaned hipster with soft hands, but here it was just practical.

"Yes, Stanley," she replied, "but don't forget I grew up here."

"That was two decades ago," he said.

"So?"

"So things have changed."

"Like how?"

He led her over to a small portion of the field near the house. It seemed different somehow. "You remember what was there?"

"The dairy. Young Billy told me already."

He nodded. "We knocked it right down. Can't imagine how Nonna kept that going so long."

"But we've still got the meat cattle out in the paddock."

"Yes," he said, "but maybe not much longer."

"Why?"

"Beef's been declining for years, but the economic recession sent prices straight down the tubes. They're almost back up now, but I'm scared off the whole idea. I mean, Scooter got it the worst. He had too much exposure to the beef market and it nearly cost him his whole operation."

Jessica remembered another benefit of cattle. "You can use the dung for fertilizer."

"We don't need the dung. Scooter sells us plenty. Oh, you wanna know another reason I want out?"

"What?"

"We grass feed them, mostly."

"The way it should be."

"But we finish them with some grain. At the last auction I went to, the word was coming down the pike that the distributors want one hundred percent grass fed." He shrugged. "They think ninety percent isn't enough."

"Nonna loves having cattle."

"That's the only reason we keep 'em." He scratched his head. "Twenty head of Hereford is just too much. I want to convince her that five or ten Dexters is a better choice."

"What are those?"

He held his hands close together. "They're small backyard cattle. Dual purpose, both milk and meat. They're getting more popular." He smirked. "But I suppose you already know all this, right, Jessica?"

She faced him. "Stanley, when are you going to stop treating me like an enemy?"

The farm manager didn't flinch. "As soon as you start

showing me you're a friend and not a burden. Now let me introduce you to the newest members of Nonna Farms."

He led her across the property past the barn, to a small enclosure. It was surrounded by a sturdy four-foot-high fence, made of welded wire. The fence was attached to seven-foot-high posts buried in concrete. Another single wire ran between the posts at human eye level.

They leaned against the fence and peered down. Inside the enclosure were seven goats, each nearly three feet high at the shoulder. They were scampering around, bursting with insane energy.

A big smile spread across Jessica's face. "I wanted Nonna to get goats when I was little. She never did."

"It took me four years to persuade her," he said.

"She really hates them."

"Oh, with a passion."

"So how did you do it?"

"I showed her the NPK of goat manure."

Jessica looked at him blankly. "What is that?"

"You don't know what that means?" His face was a mockery of accusation.

"No," she answered, "and I bet that *you* don't know what company Marc Jacobs got fired from for creating a grunge line."

"Who's Marc Jacobs?"

"Do you see my point?"

Ignoring the snark, Stanley continued the explanation. "NPK stands for nitrogen, phosphorus, and potassium. Potassium is good for veggies, but too much nitrogen can burn. Goat manure is the perfect balance. For a small farm like ours, it's almost worth its weight in gold. Nonna understood that."

Jessica felt a tugging on her jean jacket. One of the goats had thrust its snout through the hole in the wire fence and was chewing on the hem.

"Stop," she said, swatting it away.

"They'll eat anything," said Stanley. "They'll eat the produce right out of the fields. And that four-inch aperture is the biggest we can allow. Otherwise these little escape artists will strangle themselves trying to get out."

"I didn't know they were that dumb."

"Yep."

He walked a little ways down the fence towards the gate. He gestured to the latch, a complicated metal device with three different slides and knobs. "That's also why we have this. Those slippery bastards can't figure this out. So the rule is, this gate stays locked all the time, except for the two seconds we spend walking through it."

"Okay."

"I'm serious." He was looking at her firmly. "All three mechanisms must be locked."

"I heard you."

"No accidents."

Jessica felt herself growing defensive. "I grew up here."

Stanley smiled. "You keep saying that, but it sounds like something city people tell themselves to feel like they belong here." He studied her. "All right, tell you what. Let's give you your first chore and see how you handle it."

Nodding, Jessica rubbed her hands together. "Yes, please."

"Our seed supplier catalog is out of heirloom tomato seeds. They can't guarantee a shipment until next month, but we can't wait that long if we want to get them out for the season. That's the bad news. The good news is that Tommy Hackmore down said that he's got the variety we need in stock. So how about you go pick up those seeds for us?"

Jessica nodded. She hadn't been to the store in years, and this was something easy she could do immediately. It would help her to reacquaint herself with the community, to get the lay of the land, so to speak.

She pulled out her phone and opened up the notepad function. "What's the name of the variety?"

He was smiling. "Paper and pencil is too twentieth-century for you?"

"You're just as digital as anybody in the city, Stanley."

He grinned. "Fair enough."

"Tell me the name of the seed."

"It's called the Speckled Witchcackle. It's yellow. Get at least fifty packets. Our July sales depend on it."

"How should I pay?"

"We've got a line of credit."

She typed in the name, then stowed the phone away. "I'll be back in a jiffy."

"Do you know how to get there?"

"I do."

"You can take Nonna's car."

"I will."

"You say the word 'I' a lot."

Jessica paused, thinking. "The seeds will be here in one hour."

"Attagirl," he replied. "Maybe you won't embarrass yourself as badly as we thought. Have fun."

As she walked away, Jessica felt determined to prove the farm manager wrong.

Chapter Thirteen

COMING DOWN THE RISE, Jessica placed her foot on the brake and slowed down Nonna's ancient truck. Ahead was the large *faux* red barn that she'd passed the day before.

Hackmore's. The general store.

Jessica parked in the dusty lot and hesitantly turned off the engine. From inside the hood, she heard the engine rattle, sigh, then die. Twenty-three years old, outdated by at least five newer generations of vehicle, this very Ford F-150 had carried Jessica to the farm even as a child.

She didn't want to think about what it had been carrying her away from.

Jessica looked down at the dashboard. In human years, this truck was old enough to ask for the early bird menu at a restaurant. Young Billy said it took a minimum of five minutes of begging, pleading, and gentle gunning to get the engine started on cold mornings. And now, pulling the keys out, Jessica made a little prayer that this wouldn't be its last trip.

She stepped out of the truck and looked around. Above her stood the sign with the hick in the overalls chewing on the hayseed.

A group of three fifty-something farmers were leaning against the side of the store. Each one held a Styroam cup of coffee, steam rising over the brim. Their eyes coolly appraised her.

"I'm looking for Tommy," she said.

"He's here," said one.

"Where?"

"Inside."

She passed the men, feeling their eyes take in her clean hair, her fresh jeans, her pristine boots. She knew what she looked like to these men—like a young woman trying to pass herself off as competent.

"You could introduce me to him if you'd like," she said.

"Well," said one, "we don't know your name."

"It's Jessica."

"Nonna's girl?"

"Granddaughter."

He spat a mouthful of chaw into a small trash can at his feet. "Sorry to hear about her trouble."

"Thank you."

One of the men moved towards the front barn door and slid it along its tracks. Then he gestured inside.

Jessica smiled at him as she high-stepped over the track. Inside, the general store had changed. Gone were the hay bales, the dirt floor. Now it was antiseptically clean—linoleum on the floor, bright overhead lights. The aisles were packed with shelves of dry goods, animal feed, blue jeans, even some light farm equipment. A rack of lightweight trucker hats stretched behind the cash register, right next to the smokes.

It didn't feel like a turn-of-the-century rural general store anymore. It felt more like a Piggly Wiggly.

Behind her, the man cupped his hands around his mouth and shouted, "Tommy, it's Jessica. Nonna's girl."

From one of the aisles, a thin, hawklike man stepped into

frame. He wore a cotton polo shirt and a pair of old blue Wranglers. His belly was small and paunchy. He held a pricing gun in one hand.

"You're Nonna's girl?"

"Yes," she said. "Are you Tommy?"

He nodded. "Your grandma's been a good customer. Hope she's doin' better."

"She's recovering. I'm here to pitch in."

"Where from?"

"New York City." Then she quickly added: "But I grew up here."

"So what can I help you with?"

"Fifty packets of Speckled Witchcackle."

He cocked his head. "The seeds are in aisle seven."

Jessica headed over and scanned the shelving. At least thirty different types of tomato seed packets faced her. She looked through them twice, but the Speckled Witchcackle wasn't to be found.

She returned to Tommy. He was trying to hoist a large beef jerky dehydrator onto an upper shelf.

"Tommy, I can't find it."

He lowered the box unsteadily back to the floor. He turned around, his face reddened with effort, now visibly annoyed. "Well then, young lady, we're sold out."

"But Stanley said he called you this morning about it."

"It seems," he said, "we must've sold out since then."

"Do you remember selling them to anybody?"

"I don't work the register."

Jessica felt the urge to stick out her lower lip and pout, but that wouldn't endear her to anybody out here. And she *had* to succeed in this chore. After last night's mildly disastrous dinner, she couldn't fail again.

"What can I do?"

He turned back to the box. "Maybe you can see if Kilkenny has any."

"Kilkenny has a store?"

"No, he has a website. He runs it from his garage ever since his soy crop got ruined by the creek last year." Tommy paused. "We have a website too. Free shipping on orders over a hundred dollars."

"You know Nonna lives just down the road, Tommy."

"It was worth a shot."

"All right," she said, then turned to go.

"Is there anything else I can interest you in here?"

"I don't think so."

Hackmore eyed her calculatedly. "Nonna's got enough covers for the frost tonight?"

Jessica hadn't seen a weather report, but she did remember that frost killed young plants, and that farmers everywhere covered their fields on the coldest nights. In Florida, the citrus farmers even moved mobile heaters into the fields.

"Is it supposed to frost?" she asked.

"Possibly."

"I don't know if we do."

Tommy thought back. "Young Billy was telling me that he's starting ten new fifty-meter beds of Swiss chard."

"Maybe."

"I bet he doesn't have tarps yet."

"So?"

Tommy pointed to the back of the store. "Against the back wall, we've got about twelve tarps left. You buy ten, I'll throw the last two in for free. That should cover it."

Jessica knew she was being sold. But she didn't know what the farm needed. She supposed it would be better to err on the side of caution.

"What's the return policy?" she said.

Hackmore waved the question off. "Don't worry, we'll figure it out."

She shrugged. "All right then."

He headed off to the back of the store. He returned a moment later with ten large green tarps on a rolling cart.

"That's it?"

"Yep. You drive Nonna's truck?"

"Yes."

"Lemme help you put them in the bed."

She watched Tommy Hackmore wheel the cart out the front door. He loaded the tarps into the back of Nonna's truck.

Then he whipped out a receipt. Evidently he'd printed it inside. "You're all good to go, young lady. Just sign here."

She looked down. The total read $512.44.

"I didn't know tarps were that expensive."

"They're heavy," he said. "Durable. And don't forget you got two for free."

"And I can return them?"

"Sure," he said, "we'll work something out."

Jessica smiled. "Thank you."

"No, thank *you*. Your grandma's kept this store afloat for half a century."

He tipped his hat, wiped off his hands, and went back inside. On the porch, the three men with the cups of coffee had watched the whole exchange. They looked like a group of cows watching a passing train.

"Take care," she shouted.

They watched as she started up the truck and left the parking lot.

Chapter Fourteen

TEN MINUTES LATER, Jessica turned down a short dirt road with a sign marked Kilkenny's Seeds. It'd been stenciled on an old plank, but the paint was new.

She tried to recall the Kilkenny family from her childhood. Richard, the father, had been a barrel-chested man with arms like tree trunks. She did remember his great, booming laugh all these years later. The mother, Mary, was a warm but strict homemaker. They'd had three daughters, each one year apart, whose names had been lost in the fog of memory. In fact, it'd been years since Jessica had even thought of the Kilkenny family at all, though she did remember that they'd had been friendly and imaginative.

A short bridge came into view. It was made of cement and looked newly built. The truck's tires hummed smoothly for a second as she crossed it. She glanced down at the creek as it flashed by. It looked so harmless, just a brown trickle of water inside a low two-foot ditch. The idea that it could've flooded the entire field was hard to fathom.

Then she was over the bridge, back onto the dirt, the pebbles bouncing against the undercarriage of the truck. The road wound alongside the creek for a good quarter mile. Against the roof of the truck she heard the scraping of willow branches. Then the road doglegged sharply to the right, and a minute later Ainsley saw the Kilkenny homestead.

It was a simple ranch home, lowslung, in the Western style. Tall oaks shaded the house. An oil drum was leaning backwards against a wall like a movie star having a smoke. Jessica did notice that almost none of the usual farm equipment was visible. The only thing she could see was a small tractor, and that looked suspiciously clean.

Jessica parked and slipped out of her car. A sixty-something woman was on the porch in a rocking chair, mending a shirt. She was wearing a calico jumper and her hair was in a loose ponytail. Jessica liked how farm women kept their hair long as they got older.

She looked up over her spectacles, saw Jessica, then put down the needle. "A visitor," she said. "We love visitors."

"Do you remember me, Mary?" said Jessica, walking across the yard towards her.

Mary stood up from her rocking chair, came out into the cool sunlight. "I can't say that I do, but my memory is a sieve."

"I'm Jessica."

"Who?"

"Nonna's granddaughter."

Recognition dawned on her face. "Well, well. Knock me over with a feather."

Mary Kilkenny smiled. Sadly, she was proof positive that the old saying about country living, about how it kept you looking young, was not always true. Up close, Jessica could see how much Mary had aged—the gray in her hair, the crow's feet, the saggy skin.

"How long has it been, dear?" she said. "At least ten years, I figure."

"Almost twenty."

"Oh my."

Jessica shuffled her feet a little. It felt okay to be vulnerable with this woman. "Nonna's been sick."

Mary nodded. "I did hear about that. My regrets."

"She's recovering."

"That's a blessing."

"How are your girls?"

A pained expression came over Mary Kilkenny's face. "One is in Seattle, one is in Chicago, and one is stationed in Germany."

"I remember how much fun your family used to have together."

A warm smile spread over her face. "I remember too," she said quietly. "It seems like so long ago." Then she shook off the feeling like a dog flinging water after a bath. "So is this a social visit?"

"Well," replied Jessica, "I was told that you're selling seeds now."

"Yes, we've been doing that for about a year. We had to change after the storm."

"Young Billy told me that it wiped out your soy crop."

"Yes," said Mary Kilkenny. She looked down at her feet, and Jessica suddenly felt guilty that she had brought it up.

"I'm sorry, we don't have to—"

"It's all right, dear, I don't mind. Yes, that storm almost killed us. We had to liquidate almost everything just to keep the property. Now we couldn't harvest anything even if we wanted to. So we turned to seeds."

Jessica's heart went out to the woman. Nobody should have to struggle like that, late in life. "So the seed business is doing well?"

She shrugged. "At least one of our girls is helping out financially. She's the one in Chicago, a general practitioner.

Bless her heart. The other two say we should sell and move to a condo somewhere. But we can't do that."

"I don't blame you."

The woman gazed out at the willows, the creek, the fields that lay fallow. "It's like a third person in our marriage. We're wedded to the land. In good times and in bad."

Jessica felt a warmth inside. That was the essence of farming: a love of the land. Not the profit motive, not personal gain or glory. It was communion with nature.

Then Mary snapped out of her reverie. "So what's the name of this seed, dear?"

"The Speckled Witchcrackle. It's an heirloom tomato."

"The Speckled Witchcrackle." The woman thought hard. "That doesn't sound familiar."

"So you don't have it."

"Maybe Richard knows it." She turned and shouted. "Richard, come out here for a moment."

Jessica wasn't prepared for what came next. The screen door opened, and out rolled Richard in a wheelchair. He'd dropped at least forty pounds off his large frame. His head lolled unnaturally to the side.

"What's going on?" he said, slurring slightly.

"Have you heard of Speckled Witchcrackle?"

"It's a seed?"

"A tomato."

His tongue fell out of his mouth to one side while he thought about it. "No, not at all." His eyes found Jessica. "Who's this?"

"Jessica."

His face lit up. "Nonna's girl?"

"Yes."

"Nonna's doin' about as well as I am, I hear."

Jessica tried not to smile. "You've lost weight."

"That's what happens after a massive cardiac event. Six years ago."

"I'm glad you're still here," said Jessica.

"It's good to be here."

Mary, smiling at the exchange, decided to cut in. "Maybe you can call Robert's IGA. It's over in Raintree."

"Raintree?" Jessica hadn't heard of that town. "Is that near here?"

"It's about sixty miles away. Just past Springdale."

Jessica withered. She remembered where Springdale was. That would be another two hours of driving, and at least six gallons of gasoline. It wasn't her fault, or Stanley's fault either. This was Nonna's signature tomato, and according to Stanley, it was going to be worth it.

"You've been a lot of help."

"My pleasure," she said. "Stop by any time you wish."

"I will."

"Bye, Jessica," said Richard. He tried to raise his left hand. It only lifted an inch.

Jessica pulled out of the property, drove back over the bridge, and to the main road. She opened her phone to call Robert's IGA. It was out of battery. She cursed under her breath. She didn't want to go back to the Kilkennys and ask to use their telephone. Neither did she want to go back to Hackmore's. And she sure wasn't going to go back to Nonna's farm without those damn packets.

She would have to make the drive.

Chapter Fifteen

AN HOUR AND A HALF LATER, Jessica finally rolled into Raintree.

This town was different from Nonna's area. Modern consumer development had crept into its central nervous system. She'd rolled along wide boulevards with grassy medians, past Chili's, T.G.I. Friday's, Home Depot, and Wal-Mart. The brands looked odd to her, after a year and a half in New York City.

At Robert's IGA, she stepped onto black map, watched the automated doors slide open, and entered the store. She looked around. The concrete floors were glossy, the sodium lights overhead buzzed. An orange customer service sign said *Ask a sales associate for help.*

There was no need. A sales associate approached her. He was young, wearing an orange smock with a nametag that read Simon. "Hi there," he said, "what can I help you with?"

Jessica sighed and rubbed her eyes. "I need some seeds. I've driven a long ways to find them."

"If they exist, we've got 'em. Why don't you give me the names?"

"I need fifty packets of the Speckled Witchcackle."

He whipped out a notepad and jotted it down. "Type of plant?"

"Tomato."

"That's all you need?"

"Yep."

He nodded. "Okey dokey, let's head over to the kiosk."

Following him across the floor, Jessica thought about this journey. She was going to a lot of effort for some seeds. Why couldn't Stanley have used another variety? Was Nonna's farm really and truly *that* identified with the Speckled Witchcackle tomato? Would consumers really know the difference? There might be a better use of her time.

At the kiosk, Simon was standing over his computer terminal, brow furrowed, deep in concentration.

"Did you find it?" she said.

"No," he said, "it appears we don't have it."

Her heart skipped a beat. "They said that you had everything."

"We have the best selection in the region. But we don't even have a record of it in our database." He furrowed his brow and peered harder into his screen. "You said a Speckled Witchcackle?"

"Yes."

"S-p-e-c-k-l-e-d W-i-t-c-h-c-a-c-k-l-e?"

"That's what I was told."

"It's never been in this store. But I have an idea." He clicked over to another website and entered an address. "This is the Seed Savers Exchange. They're the absolute best. Based in Iowa. If they don't have it, nobody does."

Jessica waited with baited breath. "And?"

He scrolled through their website, using the search function. "There is nothing by that name. Look for yourself." He leaned to the side. "The word *Witchcackle* doesn't even bring up a result."

Jessica looked at the screen. "Holy moly."

"And look here," he said, switching to a search engine. "It doesn't bring up anything, anywhere. Are you sure the name is right?"

"Yeah," she said, "it is."

Simon straightened up, rapped his knuckles against the counter twice, and looked at her with sympathy. "Maybe you'd like to buy some other seeds? I'm partial to the Brandywine. Only eighty days to fruit."

But Jessica couldn't hear him. All she could hear was a high whine in her ears. It was the sound of fury.

She'd been tricked.

Chapter Sixteen

DURING THE DRIVE back to Nonna's farm, the world was drenched in red.

Jessica wasn't only angry. She was embarrassed, tired, and —most of all—upset with herself. She should've *known* better, her antenna should've been more attuned to possible treachery. It didn't only exist in the city.

Her right foot had grown heavier, and the truck's engine was whining as she pushed the old vehicle to its breaking point. The tachometer showed that she was nearly redlining. The body shuddered and shimmied and vibrated. She didn't care. She had only one objective.

To find Stanley.

She arrived at Nonna's farm in less than an hour. Tearing around the dirt road, she squealed to a stop in front of the farmhouse, leaped out, slammed the door. Young Billy was nearby, coiling a length of hose around a large metal spool.

He looked alarmed. "You all right?"

"Where's Stanley?"

"Out in the greenhouse. Why?"

Without answering, she walked past him. "He doesn't like to be disturbed—"

"Neither do I," she answered.

She spotted the greenhouse. A few years ago, Nonna had had enough of the old one, with its constant need for patching, and replaced the old-fashioned glass with these polycarbonate sheets, which had one-tenth the weight of glass and twice the insulation. It was a translucent hundred-foot-long structure with a peaked roof and a pair of gables at each end. Nonna said it'd been the best money she'd spent in decades.

Young Billy dropped the hose and followed her. "Well, maybe you ought to tell me the problem before you—"

Walking fast, Jessica could hear him puffing behind her. Young Billy wanted to head off a bad confrontation. She wasn't going to let him do that.

Inside, she could see a blue figure amongst the green rows. Stanley.

She found the door, which looked just like the clear panes, except it was next to a metal vent, and flung it open.

The air was a balmy seventy degrees inside, even though it was twenty degrees cooler outside. There were fifteen long rows of small green plants in brown trays. Above each row was a florescent light. Along the north wall was foil-backed bubble wrap, designed to deflect the worst of the winter winds.

Then she spotted him. Stanley was near the back of the greenhouse now, standing on a ladder, working on the wiring of one of the lamps.

He looked over at her while his hands and arms kept fixing the light.

"Hey, sweetie," he said, "you find those seeds for me?"

"No, you bastard, I did not."

Lips pursed tightly, Jessica moved firmly towards him, between the rows, through the green shoots in the brown trays.

"Why am I a bastard?"

"Because there's no such thing as a Speckled Witchcackle," she spat. "And you knew that."

The farm manager grinned, then moved slowly down the rungs and jumped onto the ground. He cleaned his hands off on his jeans. "And who finally ended your journey?"

"Robert's IGA."

He looked surprised. "In Raintree?"

"It was the third place I went."

"You could've kept looking."

"Stanley, I Googled it. You're a goddamn liar."

He was barely holding in the laughter now. Jessica grew more upset. "What's funny about wasting my whole morning? You knew exactly what you were doing."

"Which was?"

"Getting rid of me."

He shrugged. "Hey, a man's gotta have *some* peace to get any work done."

Jessica saw red drench her field of vision again. Something seized her, a violence of the type she'd never known. Her eyes scanned for something to throw at him. On the table, Stanley had left his tool box open. She reached inside, grabbed a wrench, pulled her arm back, aimed for Stanley's head—

—and felt a hand seize her wrist.

She twisted around. It was Young Billy, and his hand felt like a vise.

"There'll be no fighting in here," he said.

Shocked, she dropped the wrench. It landed on the toe of his boot. He didn't even flinch.

Young Billy let go of her hand. Then he walked around her and placed his bulk between them. Jessica hadn't noticed how mountainous a man he really was.

"I won't tolerate any wrench throwing or name-calling on this property," he said. "Understand?"

He was looking directly at Jessica. She lowered her eyes, ashamed.

"Yes," she said.

He watched her for a moment longer, to make sure that she meant it. "Okay."

Then Young Billy turned to Stanley. "Boss," he said, "you can't act like this."

"Aw, I know," he muttered.

"That's why they ran you out of the last two places."

"No they didn't."

"Yeah they did, boss."

Stanley tipped his chin up to the bigger man. "Who told you that?"

"*You* told me that."

"When?"

"When we got drunk last winter."

Stanley looked mystified. "I got drunk?"

"New Year's Day. We were snowed in with two bottles of whiskey. You told me all about how your last employer was the fundamentalist Christian family who thought that the world was invented six thousand years ago, and so you dressed up like an ape at Halloween with a sign marked *I am human* around your neck—"

Stanley had slumped against the ladder, a pained expression on his face. "So what?"

"So, I'm saying that you can be a bully. And you're being one right now to this girl." Young Billy glanced at Jessica. "Christ, think about it—she wants to *help* us. And we don't even have to *pay* her."

Stanley looked miserable. "I know it. You're right."

"Now say you're sorry."

Stanley looked at Jessica. "I'm sorry."

"Dammit," said Young Billy, knocking Stanley's hat off his head, "be a gentleman and say it like you mean it."

His unkempt head exposed, Stanley repeated himself. "Jessica, I'm sorry for sending you on a wild goose chase. Please accept my apology."

Jessica felt the angry thrumming in her head begin to slow itself down. "Your apology is accepted."

The trio stood there in awkward silence.

"Now what?" said Stanley.

"I guess I should mention that I bought something for us at Hackmore's," she said.

"What's that?"

"Something that Tommy said we'd need."

A look of skepticism appeared on Stanley's face. "What?"

"Tarps."

"Frost tarps?"

She nodded. "Twelve of them. But he gave me two extra for free, so we only paid for ten."

Stanley's eyes searched her face. She didn't know for what. Young Billy was standing very still, holding his breath.

"We," said Stanley, "don't need any tarps."

"Tommy said you planted ten new fifty-meter beds of Swiss chard."

Young Billy held up a hand. "Now, wait a minute. I told him that we were *thinking* of it. We haven't done it yet."

"How much did he charge you?" asked Stanley.

"Five hundred dollars."

The farm manager staggered back, clutching his heart dramatically. "You put five hundred dollars on our line of credit at that store?"

"It's no big deal," said Jessica, trying to play it casual. "Besides, they're heavy-duty plastic."

Young Billy rubbed his forehead, while Stanley howled. "Tommy sold you *plastic* tarps? For five hundred dollars?"

She was panicking now. "He said we could return them if we wanted."

"Were those his words exactly?"

Jessica thought back. "He said that we could work something out and—"

Young Billy interrupted her. "Jessica, number one, we don't need any tarps. I never planted that Swiss chard, and Tommy knows it too. Number two, we don't need plastic, that's for sure. Number three, Tommy isn't going to issue a refund."

Stanley held a theatrical hand against his forehead. "Since his daddy died, he's been squeezing this community for everything he can. In fact, I think he's planning to close the store." He blew air out of his cheeks. "That five hundred dollars is gone."

"But he thanked me for Nonna's fifty years of support—"

"That's just talk. He's a user."

Young Billy nodded. "You'll have better luck taking a fish from a grizzly than getting that five hundred dollars back."

Jessica deflated. She'd been so sure that she was helping her grandmother, but these men viewed her as just another silly girl from the city who went on a shopping spree with somebody else's credit card—and that was precisely the opposite of how she wanted to be seen.

"Look, don't feel bad," said Young Billy. "I know you were trying to do the right thing."

"Yeah, we'll use the tarps for something, eventually," said Stanley.

"Are you sure?" she said.

"Positive." Young Billy smiled and squeezed her underneath his armpit. She smiled back.

Chapter Seventeen

THAT AFTERNOON, Stanley confirmed the frost forecast, and the four began gearing up for a long night. Jessica and Ernesto were tasked with the job of pulling the tarps over the beans, lettuce, carrots, eggplants, and summer squash.

This how, at three in the afternoon, she found herself walking down the long rows of barely sprouted squash with a long water hose, spraying the plants by hand. The water helped prevent frost, a surprise to Jessica.

Behind her walked Ernesto, carrying a stack of burlap tarps. Stanley had explained that plastic actually could damage the plants the next day by overheating them.

"*Aqui*?" she said.

He nodded.

They stopped, spread the burlap over the plants, then drove a thin metal stake through each of the four corners of the burlap into the soil.

"*Donde de*?" she said.

Ernesto's brown eyes flicked up at her, then back down. He said nothing. He had thick lips and high cheekbones. It was a feminine face, in contrast with the grubby farmhand clothing.

"*No quieras decir*?" she said. She was grateful for her high school Spanish.

He squeezed out the next three words as though it physically pained him. "Let's just work."

Jessica noticed that he didn't have a strong accent. In fact, he sounded nearly American. That meant that he had some mental flexibility. He certainly had intelligent eyes.

He stood up and returned to fetch another stack of burlap tarps. Jessica continued spraying the rows with water.

Across the field, Young Billy was approaching. "You won't ever hear Stanley tell you this," he said, stepping across the rows, "but it turns out that we misjudged the number of tarps. We're gonna have to use those twelve you bought."

Jessica smiled. "That's good to hear."

"But don't tell Stanley," he said.

"I won't."

He peered at their work. "At this rate, you'll finish just before sunset. And don't forget to bring in the rain gauge. We don't want it to freeze."

By sundown, Jessica had watered most of the property and with Ernesto had hammered most of the tarps into the ground. By the end, they'd run out of stakes and were just flinging the fabric across the plants.

Now, hobbling back to the house, Jessica felt the aching in the twin muscles that ran up along her spine. This was dull and uninteresting work—crouching, standing, spraying, crouching, hammering. It was the type of labor, like housecleaning, that was oddly strenuous, the type that took its toll on your body after years. She wondered how Nonna had managed for so long.

She staggered inside, kicked off her boots, and fell onto the living room couch. Young Billy and Stanley entered a moment later. "We did it. Everything's secured."

"These damn frosts," said Stanley. "It's April. I thought we'd seen the last of them."

"Weather's changin'," said Young Billy.

They took off their hats and shoes, then looked down at Jessica. Her mouth had fallen open, and she was snoring.

"Jessica," said Young Billy.

No response.

He walked over and gently shook her toe. Jessica's eyes flew open. "What?"

"You did a good job in the field today," he said.

"Thanks."

She lifted her head. Their eyes were imploring her. She dropped her head backwards. They wanted dinner. For the last twelve hours, she'd been going, going, going. She hadn't even thought about the meal. But she'd promised her grandmother that she would cook.

"I was thinking about what to make," she lied, "and I've just figured it out."

Groaning, she pulled herself to her feet and staggered into the kitchen.

"Do you want any help?" said Young Billy.

"No," she said.

"I don't really want McDonald's again."

"It'll be good this time."

A half-hour later, she had boiled pasta and was frantically trying to defrost a log of frozen ground beef for the sauce. She was holding it under a stream of hot water in the sink. Only the outer layer of meat had warmed, but her fingers were completely numb.

Young Billy came in. "Looks like you're still having trouble."

"I forgot to pull this out of the freezer this morning."

"Maybe you should start meal planning," he said.

He was right, but Jessica didn't want him to know that. "Maybe," she said.

"Can I help?"

"Nonna said you don't cook. At all."

Young Billy went to the other sink, squirted Lava soap into his hands, and scrubbed them. "That," he said, "is because she refuses to give up control of her kitchen."

"Really."

"She tells us we can't do anything so that we don't challenge her authority."

"So you *do* cook?"

He shrugged. "Maybe a little."

She nodded at the cutting board. "You can start by prepping the sauce."

He went over to the board, peeled the garlic head into its cloves, put them on a plate, and shoved them in the small microwave.

Jessica watched him, panicked. Maybe there was a very good reason that Nonna hadn't allowed him in the kitchen. "You can't microwave garlic," she said.

The microwave dinged. He pulled out the plate and proceeded to squeeze each garlic clove with a brisk pinch between his thumbs. The garlic popped out easily.

"Wow," she said, "I've never seen that."

"It's an old trick. The heat separates the garlic from the wrapper. I see it happen out in the fields after a week of ninety-five degrees."

"We grow garlic too?"

"Jessica, there is nothing we haven't grown."

They worked side-by-side. She noticed Young Billy's fine handiwork on the cutting board. He chopped tomatoes with astonishing speed. He didn't waste a single movement.

"That's it," she said. "I need to know the truth."

He grinned. "I was a sous chef a long time ago."

"I thought you spent your whole life here on the farm."

"No," he said, "I left for a couple of years. Went to the city. Didn't like it so much."

"And Nonna still doesn't let you cook."

He shrugged. "She's territorial. Would you like to watch?"

She took off her apron, leaned against the wall, and watched Young Billy assemble the sauce, let it simmer, then pour it over the pasta. She watched him assemble a heavy farmhouse salad with black olives, more tomatoes, thick shavings of Parmesan cheese, and a homemade dressing.

"Can you teach me how to do all that?" she said.

"Sure."

"Really?"

"Of course. Then I won't have to cook. Now let's eat. Grab those plates."

A mischievous glimmer danced in his eyes as he passed her. Jessica followed to the table, thoroughly humbled.

Chapter Eighteen

THAT NIGHT, Jessica lay on her bed in the attic, swaddled in blankets, shivering. Her every exhalation was making a great frosty breath in the air in front of her.

This room wasn't anything like she'd remembered. The attic had been her childhood bedroom for two years, and it'd been the coziest place she'd ever lived—teddy bears, small table for art projects, bedside lamp, fluffy down comforter. It'd been the ultimate little girl's room.

Or had it?

Maybe it was a trick of memory. After all, Nonna had brought her to the farm to escape an awful situation. A sewer pipe probably would've seemed like heaven by comparison.

Right now, however, Jessica could definitely pinpoint the source of the problem: There was a hole in the roof. From her bed, it was about the size of a small dinner plate. Through it, she could see the white stars twinkling in the black sky. Last night she hadn't noticed it, since she'd passed out so quickly. But tonight was much colder, thanks to the frost, and the tip of Jessica's nose was frozen.

She pulled the blanket over her face and allowed herself to

think about her mother, the woman with a past so miserable and checkered that she could've been, should've been, a poster child for the dangers of the entire nineteen-seventies. Jessica never knew that decade, but she had gotten a taste of its excesses.

A rolled-up bill here.

White powdery residue on a mirror there.

A blurry parade of men through the front door.

As an adult, in New York, she'd made a few visits to a therapist, a polite but steely older woman who'd asked a few tentative questions about her childhood. Jessica hadn't really felt ready to open up to her, so she'd talked instead about something else.

Nonna's farm. Her happy place.

Jessica threw the blankets off herself. There would be no sleep in here tonight. The room was too cold, her mind too wracked.

She stood up, wrapped a bathrobe around herself, then went down the creaky stairs to the main floor. A thin line of yellow light shone under Nonna's bedroom door.

She knocked hesitantly on her door. "Nonna?"

"Yes," came the old woman's voice.

She pushed open the door. Her grandmother was tucked into her bed, reading a book. She looked at Jessica over the wire rims of her eyeglasses. "You can't sleep either?"

Jessica shook her head.

Nonna closed the book and put it facedown on the nightstand. Jessica saw that it was a bodice ripper. She smiled. Nonna wasn't the type to admit to much need for romance.

"I sleep whenever my body tells me to," said Nonna. "It's out of my control."

"The attic is really cold. There's a hole in the roof."

Nonna looked into the distance. For a moment she seemed determined to climb out of bed and fix the roof immediately.

"I was going to take care of that," she said quietly. "Before this."

Jessica slid into bed with her grandmother. "Am I too big to lay here?"

"Heavens, no." Nonna lifted an arm and put it around her granddaughter. "Do you remember doing this when you were little?"

"Yes."

Jessica looked at the landscape painting on the wall. It was her grandmother's favorite. It'd been painted by her grandfather in his spare time. Everyone said it'd been merely a late-in-life hobby, but Jessica thought that the brush strokes and the control of shading showed a professionalism that had never been appreciated.

"Do you ever get tired of looking at that?"

"Of course not. It was Samuel's very best. His soul is in that canvas."

"I wish I could've met him."

"You did. You were six months old."

"I don't remember."

They lay in silence for a long while. Then Nonna said, "Young Billy told me about the wild goose chase that Stanley sent you on."

"Yeah."

"He did the same to Ernesto on his first day."

"Stanley," said Jessica, "is an asshole."

"Maybe a little. But he's good at what he does. He's saved this farm a lot of money."

Nonna coughed a little. Her body seemed frail, much more so than ever before. Jessica had always admired her grandmother for her sheer physicality. She had the constitution of an ox. People often used the phrase *never been sick a day in her life*, but in Nonna's case it was literally true. Minus coughs and colds, this was the first time she'd ever been down for any length of time, ever.

"It's weird seeing you stuck in bed, Nonna," said Jessica.

"It does feel strange," she replied. "I guess I saved all the up, dear."

"I saw the Kilkennys today. They said hello."

"They're still hangin' on," said Nonna. "There but for the grace of God go I."

"Not being next to the creek helps."

"True."

"Richard's not doing so well, is he?"

Nonna shook her head. "I really thought they were going to sell after his heart attack. But they'd rather not. I bought some of their goods at auction. We all bid up the items too, just to do them a favor."

Jessica laid her head on her grandmother's shoulder. "I don't know if I'm going to help the farm or hurt it."

"You," tutted her grandmother, "are a capable young woman. The adjustment will be difficult, though."

"I know."

"And anytime you need to talk, just come to me. I'll be here for you. Okay?"

There was no response.

"Jessie?"

Nonna angled her head and looked down at her grand-daughter. Jessica was already asleep.

Chapter Nineteen

THE NEXT MORNING, Jessica entered the kitchen in a robe, yawning. She gazed blearily at the old appliances, at the pantry packed with staples, at the cast-iron pans handing from hooks above the six-top burner.

It was time to make breakfast.

"Don't bother," said a voice. It was Stanley, standing in the doorway. He was dressed in a collar shirt and chinos and dress shoes. "Nonna wants to go to church. We're leaving in an hour."

"It's Sunday?"

"Yep."

She'd lost track of the days. Jessica glanced around. "But I'm hungry."

"Good to see you developing a farmhouse appetite."

Jessica nodded. She'd never eaten breakfast in New York. A cup of yogurt, at most, with a little bit of coffee to wash it down, and always on the sidewalk, or at her desk. Things had changed.

"So where are we going to eat?"

"At the pancake breakfast after service."

"I'd better dress up."

"If you want."

Jessica retreated upstairs and opened her suitcase. From the moment she'd arrived at the farm, she'd been too busy to even unpack.

She dumped her clothing out on her bed and picked out a few finalists. After modeling in the full-length free-standing oval mirror, the same one she'd played dressup in as a child, she settled on a purple A-line number. It was demure enough to be worn to her job, but the color was bright enough that she'd gotten compliments on it.

In the bathroom, she opened her makeup case. This was another question entirely. How much should she apply for a Sunday morning church service in a rural county? Less was probably more. She applied some foundation, a little blush, and some eyeliner. That was enough.

Onto shoes. Jessica only owned nine pairs. This wasn't very much, at least by city standards, but she hadn't been able to afford any of the fashionable brands that she'd been taught to covet. The bloom was off that rose anyways. She selected a pair of black closed-toe heels.

Downstairs, Nonna was in the middle of the driveway, leaning on her walker, Young Billy and Stanley were standing around her. Jessica hadn't seen her upright since her stroke. It wasn't easy to see her grandmother like this.

"You look good," said Nonna.

"So do you."

She rolled her eyes. "Please."

Young Billy opened the door and helped Nonna ease herself into the passenger seat. "There you go," he said.

"Oh boy," she said, "that's not as easy as it used to be."

"We don't have to go."

Nonna looked up at him, resolve glinting in her blue eyes. *"I'm going to church."*

"Yes, ma'am."

Jessica and Stanley slipped into the backseat of the extended cab. Then Young Billy slipped behind the wheel and started the engine and turned the truck out towards the road.

As the dirt sang under their feet, Stanley looked over at Jessica's outfit. "That's a nice dress."

"Thank you."

"I don't know what the congregation is going to think, though."

"Why?"

"Purple is for eggplants and bruises out here."

Jessica laughed. "Well, maybe I'll push the congregation a little."

"You can try, but if it isn't pastels and pearls, they don't know it."

A half-hour later, they pulled into the parking lot of the church. A modern structure, it boasted front and rear gables made of glass. Jessica could see straight through the church, through to the cornfields beyond.

Inside, they found seats near the back, where a few hundred people had already congregated in the long seats. Most of the men were dressed in freshly laundered polo shirts and had short, crisp haircuts. They sat with arms crossed, stoic expressions on their faces.

The women were equally plain. Each wore a different pale blouse, most with pearls, as Stanley had noted. Everyone wore skirts that reached to midway down their calves. Jessica tugged her knee-length skirt down a little bit.

As she looked around, she noticed something else that was odd.

There were almost no children.

"Where are the kids?" she whispered to her grandmother.

"The community has lost a lot of its young families," said Nonna.

The music started up, and the choir arrived in their robes. The songs were joyful but restrained.

Later, the preacher arrived onstage. He was a lanky man dressed in a blue collared shirt and gray dress slacks. He scanned the audience before beginning his homily.

"One thing to remember," he said, "is that the Lord works in mysterious ways. These ways are not absent. They're merely *unknown* to us. So our task is to remember Jesus, even when you think he's forgotten you. Because he hasn't. Only then will the Lord find you." He paused, his eyes landing upon Jessica. "You don't need to wrap yourself in a bright purple dress for the Lord to notice you."

Jessica saw hundreds of heads swivel around to notice her. She shrank down in her seat.

"But you can't hide, neither," said the preacher, growing more animated now. "God finds all of his creatures."

Jessica didn't listen to the rest of the message. Her mind was too wracked with self-consciousness, and regret for her choice of color.

After the service had ended, they helped Nonna to her feet and made their way outside. Jessica noticed the other women looking at her with amusement.

"I told you that was a nice dress," whispered Stanley.

"Shut up," she said.

Chapter Twenty

THE PANCAKE BREAKFAST was held in the gymnasium of the middle school down the street.

The wooden floor of the basketball court had been covered with white plastic sheeting. Long rows of benches and tables awaited, with sets of plasticware and napkins spaced out nicely on the paper tablecloth.

At the far end of the gym, underneath a basketball hoop, four large flattop stoves were being manned by four large male cooks. Each one was in constant motion, ladling batter from a large container onto the flat skillet.

Jessica stood in line at the first station, two plates in hand, watching the cook. He was about her age, fairly attractive, nice and charming. He was joking with a pair of elderly women. She sized him up. He had potential, but the only problem was that he was carrying about twenty extra pounds around his midsection. It was a problem everywhere these days.

Jessica stepped to the front of the line, and he glanced her up and down. "I'm guessing two pancakes."

"Four," she said.

"Big appetite."

"Two are for my grandmother."

"Ah, a girl who loves her family. Rarer than a unicorn."

He poured two pools of batter on the flattop, and Jessica melted a little. "That's very nice of you to say. What's your name?"

"I'm Mike. Who's your grandmother?"

"Nonna."

The cook froze. "Wait—are you *Jessica*?"

"Yes."

He grew visibly nervous. "You don't remember me?"

Jessica eyed him, tried to imagine fifteen pounds off the midsection. He still didn't ring a bell.

"No, sorry."

"It's me—*Mikey*."

Mikey. She repeated the name to herself—

—then saw his face rising out of the misty depths of childhood memory.

"Mikey?" she said. "We used to—"

"—play together when we were six? Remember?"

Then it hit her. She'd known Mikey very well. In fact, they'd been best friends for one short summer, her last one on the farm. They'd played in the creeks, swam in ponds, played hide-and-seek in the tall August cornfields. It was one of those blessed friendships that a boy and a girl can only have during a short window of time, before hormones change the game completely.

"Oh my God," she said.

He was grinning now, pouring more batter onto the flattop. "How'va ya been?"

"I don't ... it's just ... my gosh, there's so much to say. What are you doing now?"

"Pancake chef. Full time."

An astonished look appeared on her face. "Just kidding," he said. "I work for AgriCon."

Jessica knew that name. It was one of the giant agribusiness interests that had purchased a lot of land in the area. If you were going to sell the farm, this corporation would almost certainly be the buyer—and many people had taken advantage.

But it was reviled. To increase crop yields, AgriCon had pummeled its soils with tank upon tank, silo upon silo, of nitrogen and ammonia. While Nonna hadn't kept her farm totally free of fertilizer, she had used it judiciously, resisting the kind of carpetbombing that destroyed good soil and left ponds full of algae blooms. AgriCon had never shown such restraint.

But Jessica stayed diplomatic. "How's that going for you?"

"Good paycheck. Don't have to worry."

She nodded.

"I heard Reverend Tom called out somebody in purple," he said. "I'm guessing that was you."

Jessica shook her head. "Next week I'm wearing an old lady outfit."

"No, don't," he said. "I like it."

"Thank you."

"Besides, some of these old people are threatened by attractive young women."

Jessica smiled. It felt odd to flirt here, so far from the city —and yet, for that very reason, the conversation seemed better. In fact, everything carried more meaning when there was less of it, especially words.

He slipped another pancake onto her other plate. "Tell Nonna this one was made with an extra helping of love."

"I will."

"She's a tough woman."

"A survivor."

He nodded.

Jessica carried the pancakes over to her grandmother and

sat down beside her. "Nonna, do you know who that is?" she said.

"Who?"

"The man on the stove. On the far left."

Nonna peered across the gymnasium. "The heavy one?"

"Yes."

"Heavens, I can't see his face."

"That's Mikey."

She watched her grandmother's face for a reaction.

"Little Mikey?" said Nonna.

"Yep."

"Good Lord, he's bigger."

"I know."

Nonna frowned. "He used to be so skinny. Maybe somebody's cooking well for him. Is he married?"

"I don't know."

Her grandmother sliced into her pancake. "We couldn't pry you two apart that one summer."

Jessica nodded. As she poured syrup onto her pancakes, and as locals wandered over to congratulate Nonna on surviving her illness, Jessica watched the cook. He was laughing, teasing, flipping pancakes. He seemed so sure of himself, of his place in this community.

She said his name again. *Mikey*.

Chapter Twenty-One

THE SUN CRACKING over the horizon, Jessica was kneeling in the cold dirt, reaching into the rear door of the chicken coop.

It was six-thirty am, Monday morning, and she'd just finished cooking a farmhouse breakfast. She was starting to get the hang of it. Fresh scrambled eggs, slabs of buttered toast, thick slices of bacon. Nonna had explained that farmwork required lots of calories, that excess fat wasn't a worry here.

Now she had been summoned by Young Billy to her first job of the morning.

Chickens.

The chicken coop was shaped like a large barn, about twenty feet long by ten feet wide. It was a wooden structure with a corrugated metal roof. Mesh wire completely encased the open sides and the bottom. Roosting bars stretched from one side to the other.

And it was on wheels.

Jessica unlatched the egg door and swung it down. Inside were the rear ends of fourteen hens, sitting in straw nests.

They immediately started singing. *Cack-cack-cack-cack-OOOOOOO.*

"That's good news," said Young Billy, standing behind her. "Singing means the hens are laying."

Jessica stared at them, the handle of the bucket feeling warm in her hand.

"Don't be shy," he said.

"But what if they peck at me?"

He smiled. "Oh, worse things have happened. Besides, you'll learn to spot the mean ones pretty quick."

Jessica tentatively reached underneath a hen's behind. Through the thin rubber of her disposable glove, her fingers felt something smooth, oval, and warm.

She pulled it out and looked at it. It was an egg. As simple as that. And yet somehow profound.

She placed it gently into the bucket, then moved onto the second hen. She reached under the animal more boldly. There were two eggs. She withdrew them one at a time. They were soft. One even had a bit of blood, which she wiped off.

"Good," said Young Billy.

She moved onto the third hen. This one turned its head sideways, watching Jessica out of the side of its face.

Then it pecked Jessica's arm. Hard.

Jessica yelped and leaped back. Young Billy laughed. "That's a mean one. Ernesto hates her."

Soon Jessica had harvested fifteen eggs from the coop. She closed the egg hatch and latched it tightly. "Now the next coop?"

To her left were three more identical chicken coops, all in a straight row. Each one held about twenty-five hens, for a total of one hundred. Many of them laid eggs every day, which meant that they were harvesting over five hundred eggs a week. Selling them at the farmers' market had been a long-standing part of Nonna's business plan.

"No, Ernesto already did the other three," answered Young Billy. "We saved this one for you to practice."

"So now we're finished?"

"Now you have to move the coop."

"To where?"

He pointed to a spot on the grass, about thirty feet away. "Right there."

"Why?"

"So they can fertilize another part of the ground."

The scheme dawned on Jessica. "And that's why you have mesh on the bottom."

Young Billy nodded. "We just pick up the coop and move 'em."

"Every day?"

"Rain or shine."

She walked around the chicken coop to the front. A hitch was affixed to the front of the structure. On either side were two rubber handles.

"How much does it weigh?"

Young Billy shrugged. "Maybe two hundred pounds."

"So you use the tractor, right?"

He ruffled the back of his hair. "I guess we could, but driving it over here and hooking up the hitch takes too long. Especially for four different coops. It's easier just to drag it by hand."

"But I'm not strong enough do that."

"Sure you are."

Jessica looked at the coop. "It's at least two hundred pounds."

"It's on wheels," said Young Billy. "The hardest part is at the beginning. After that, the momentum carries most of it. Go on, try."

Frowning, Jessica grabbed the handles and lifted. The

coop felt even heavier than she'd expected. She managed to hoist the mesh about an inch or two off the grass.

"Now walk," he said.

"Backwards?"

"It's only thirty feet."

Straining, she began shuffling her feet backwards. The rubber wheels at the back of the coop were turning. From inside the coop came an anguished squawking and the anxious flutter of wings.

"Ignore them," said Young Billy. "You're almost there."

Jessica's arms were beginning to tire. She didn't know how much longer she could hold it up.

"And ... stop," said Young Billy.

Jessica dropped the coop with a crash. The whole wooden structure shook. Twenty chickens came flapping out of the protected area and down into the new grass.

"Oh my God, I hurt them."

"Nope. It's hard to hurt a chicken in its coop. Look, they're happy."

The chickens were already down on the earth, pecking away, looking for new blades of grass, small bugs, juicy worms, bits of hay.

Jessica stood there, panting. "Nonna did the chickens differently when I was a kid."

Young Billy refilled the chickens' water and feed troughs. "We've come a long ways. Turns out that cramming four thousand chickens into mile-long sheds and making them live in their own feces actually *didn't* improve the quality of food."

"Makes sense."

"So do you like this chore?"

Jessica nodded. "It's kind of interesting. But I don't think that I can drag four of these coops thirty feet every morning."

"Well, you're going to find out." Young Billy straightened up. "The chickens are all yours, starting tomorrow morning."

Jessica smiled. She was feeling excited that she would have some responsibilities on the farm.

"Bring it on," she said.

Then she glimpsed a figure moving towards them across the field of alfalfa and clover. It was Stanley.

"Hey," shouted Young Billy, "Jessica got her first taste of success here. She took the eggs and moved the coop. All by herself."

"That's wonderful," said Stanley, his voice dripping with sarcasm, "but it's too bad she hasn't learned to listen to me."

Jessica noticed him carrying a long piece of gray plastic in his hand. As he drew nearer, she could see that the end of the object was broken and jagged. It seemed to have exploded.

Stanley tossed the object at her feet. "Look at that."

"What is it?" said Jessica.

"That's the rain gauge," he said. "You left it out in the field during the frost, and the water inside froze. When water freezes, it expands. So now it burst the gauge. It's broken."

Jessica blanched. She remembered him telling her to bring that in before the frost. She'd forgotten. Now she was in trouble.

Jessica crouched and picked up the pieces. "I'm really sorry."

"You should be."

Young Billy tried to step between them. "It's not an expensive item, Stanley."

"That's not the point."

"Then what is the point?"

"Personal responsibility for one's mistakes." He pointed at Jessica. "I want you to buy a new one. With *your* money. Not ours."

The manager stalked away.

Young Billy slid his eyes around sideways to Jessica. "Don't worry too much," he said, "we all make mistakes."

Jessica felt embarrassment knifing through her. "But I make a lot of them."

"Tell you what. I'll move the other coops, and you go buy a new one. And use your money so he doesn't get upset."

"Okay."

As she left the fields, Jessica realized that learning farm life was one step forward, two steps back.

Chapter Twenty-Two

JESSICA PEELED down the road and arrived at Hackmore's store. The same three farmers were arranged outside the front door, coffee steam swirling up from the Styrofoam cups in their hands. She wondered if they ever worked.

She was aware of them watching her as she stepped out of the farm truck.

"Good morning," she said.

"Mornin'," replied one. "Seems like you found Tommy the other day."

"I did."

She stood before them, pulling her hair back into a pony-tail. The three men watched her closely. To them, seeing a young city girl out stepping out of a truck at a feed store was like watching a poodle walk on its hind legs.

"What are you looking for this time?" said the one.

"A rain gauge."

He nodded solemnly. "Forgot to bring it in during the frost?"

"Yep."

He nodded towards the interior of the store. "They're in the back."

"Thanks."

She started to move inside. "Hey," the one said.

Jessica stopped. "What?"

"Watch out for Tommy."

"Yeah, I kind of learned that already."

The three men were grinning now. "He upsold you on the tarps pretty good, didn't he," said the one.

"Yeah," she said. "But we used them all, actually."

She walked inside, feeling embarrassed. It seemed that she had been the topic of local conversation. The people had probably been laying bets on how long the city girl would last before leaving.

It made her angry.

Inside, Hackmore's was quiet. Behind the register, a teenage girl was pecking moodily at her smartphone.

"Hi," said Jessica.

"Hi," she replied.

"Rain gauges?"

The girl set down her phone, annoyed. "Dad, where's the rain gauges?"

From a nearby aisle stepped Tommy, the same pricing gun in his hand. "They're in the back." Then he saw Jessica. "Oh, hey there. How'd those tarps work out?"

Jessica pretended to be searching for something in her purse. "Just fine, thank you."

"You need some help finding that rain gauge?"

"No, I'll get it myself."

She heard Tommy walking behind her as she went to the back of the store. She found the long gray plastic tube with the clear tip. It was the exact same one that Stanley had thrown at her feet.

"That's twenty-nine ninety-nine," he said.

She verified the price sticker. It read $29.99. "You don't have anything cheaper?"

Tommy shook his head. "That's the only one."

"I'll take it."

"All right."

He trailed her back to the register and went around the counter. "Move," Tommy told his daughter.

"She can ring me up," said Jessica.

"No, no," he said, "I'll handle your purchase. Is there anything else you need today?"

Jessica could sense him angling for something. "No thank you," she said.

"Some animal feed?"

"We're fine."

"Need some new jeans?"

"Nope."

He rang up her purchase. "That'll be thirty-two forty with tax. I'll put it on Nonna's account and—"

Jessica stopped him. "No, I'd like to pay for this personally."

Tommy paused, regarding her over the thin wire rims of his glasses. "Personally?"

"Yes, with a credit card."

"We don't accept credit cards anymore."

"Why?"

"The merchant fees. Staying PCI compliant is damn near impossible for a small business like this. They have everything but a gun in their hands."

Jessica shrugged. She had a little over fifty dollars in her wallet. "Then let's do cash."

He held his palms up and shied away backwards, as though she were waving a flaming torch at his midsection.

"Uh, I can't take that," he said.

"You can't take *cash*?"

She could see his eyes shifting. "I mean, uh, I could, but, uh ... you'd have to open a new personal account first."

"Okay."

"That costs two hundred dollars."

"To open an *account*?"

He hemmed and hawed. "See, it would be a personal account under your name, but we have to set it up as a business account."

He smiled at her wanly, a grotesque imitation of customer service. In her mind, Jessica's bullcrap meter began to sound at top volume.

"This is ridiculous," she said. "I can't pay with credit, and yet it will cost two hundred to open a store account."

He shrugged.

"This business isn't very customer-friendly."

"I'm sorry you feel that way."

Jessica decided to be more direct. "Are you planning to keep this business?"

His eyes zeroed in on her. "What does that mean?"

"Because you're pissing off the community. Cutting corners, squeezing people."

"This business has been in my family for *generations*," Tommy said. His daughter glanced at him worriedly as his voice rose. "And I resent *outsiders* like *you* coming in here and telling *me* how to run *my* business."

"Everybody loved your father," said Jessica.

"I know that."

"You're squandering that love."

His daughter interjected. "Grandpa didn't charge two hundred dollars to open an account, Dad."

"You," he said, "will shut your mouth right now."

Jessica looked sympathetically at his daughter, who had turned moodily back to her phone.

"Look," Jessica said, "the short story is that I'm not buying this rain gauge."

His face was made of steel. "That's your choice."

"In fact, Nonna isn't buying anything from you ever again," she continued, "until you change the way you run this business."

"We'll see," he said.

"We will."

Jessica spun on her heel and left the store.

The three men out front watched her go. "Have a nice morning," one said.

Chapter Twenty-Three

JESSICA WARILY PLUNKED the ladder against the side of her grandmother's farmhouse, then looked up at the roof. Her mission was clear.

She was going to fix the hole in the roof. The one above the attic, where she was sleeping. Young Billy hadn't given her any new assignments since coming back from the store, and she wasn't going to bother him every minute of every hour. She was going to make herself *useful*.

Jessica slung a plastic bag over her shoulder. It was filled with all sorts of old farm rags that she'd found in the utility shed. They were stiff and crinkled with dried mud, perfect for stuffing in the hole. She also had a wide, flat rock that she'd picked up over near the orchard that morning.

It would be a short-term fix, and probably wouldn't last through the next rainstorm, but at least she was taking charge.

Around her a couple of the farmhouse dogs were running, barking, nipping at one another. They were strong tubes of muscle, at least eighty pounds each, and when they played, they played hard.

"Get out of here," she said.

One barked happily at her. Then the other tackled him, and the tussling continued.

Ignoring them, Jessica plunked her left foot on the first rung and stepped up. The ladder teetered a little. The feet of the ladder weren't driving into the dirt because it was still hardened from the winter. In the fall, her weight on the ladder would've driven it into the soil

She stepped to the second rung, then the third. The ladder wobbled slightly, and she grew nervous.

When she'd reached the top of ladder, she carefully placed her right foot onto the overhang. The brown shingles felt old and brittle beneath her boot. Then she swung her weight around and rolled fully onto the roof of the farmhouse.

She looked around. The roof was gently sloped, with at least a quarter of the shingles missing, bits of leaves and dirt encrusted beneath the remaining ones. Nonna needed to do some serious work up here, but that was another expense that she couldn't afford right now.

Scanning the surface, Jessica quickly spotted the hole a few feet away. She approached lightly, guessing the stability of the surrounding roof would be weakened. She lowered to her hands and knees, feeling the rough sandpaper texture under her palms, and crawled slowly to the edge of the damage.

The hole was a bit wider than her arm and plunged down about two feet to the ceiling of the attic. Producing the rags, she quickly stuffed them into the crevice, pushing them into the hole, cramming them as tightly as possible without pushing them all the way through. Then she produced the flat, heavy stone from the pack and laid it across the hole.

When she was done, she regarded her handiwork. It was a rookie fix, a temporary job, but decent.

Satisfied, Jessica crawled backwards, got to her feet, and carefully moved back towards the ladder. Then she heard the sound of metal crashing into dirt.

The ladder was gone.

Panicking, she approached the edge of the roof and looked down. The ladder was laying sideways on the dirt. Around the ladder were circling the farm dogs, looking startled. One of them sniffed it suspiciously.

Their roughhousing had just knocked over the ladder.

"You two," she said, "are a couple of jerks."

The dogs looked up at her, tails wagging. One barked happily. They thought this was a game.

"Go get Young Billy," she said.

The dogs tilted their heads, listening, but didn't move.

"*Go get Young Billy*," she repeated. "Go on."

One of the dogs barked happily, circled twice, then lay down in the dirt. The other one followed. They'd tired themselves out.

Swearing under her breath, Jessica crossed to the other side of the roof and peered out into the fields. Below her was the goat enclosure, the greenhouse, and out beyond that, the tiny figure of Stanley in the pasture, almost a quarter mile away. She turned around. In the other direction, the tiny figure of Young Billy was washing out some bins at the auxiliary pump down the dirt road, near the entrance. He liked to use that one for cleaning because it was far from the house's water supply.

Both were too far away for shouting, and Jessica hadn't been issued a radio yet. Nonna was in the house below her, of course, but she spent most of the day asleep.

Jessica realized that she was most likely going to spend the whole morning marooned on this roof until someone noticed that she was gone.

Then she heard a slam from the shed. She ran across the roof, avoiding the hole. The shed door was open. Someone was rummaging inside.

Then Ernesto emerged, carrying a coil of rope around his right shoulder.

From the roof, Jessica studied him as he started to cross the yard. Ernesto wasn't tall, but he'd been blessed with a barrel chest. Even from here, she could see his muscles straining against his t-shirt. The fieldhand also carried himself with quiet pride, even now, when he thought that nobody was watching.

As he passed directly below her, Jessica decided to blow her position. She cupped her hands around her mouth.

"Ernesto," she shouted.

The fieldhand stopped and looked around, his demeanor instantly wary, protective.

"Up here," she said.

He craned his head upwards and covered his eyes with his hand, shielding them from the sun.

"*Como*?" he said.

"The ladder fell down," she replied. "Can you help? *Ayudar*?"

Ernesto dropped the coiled rope, then spotted the ladder in the dirt. He shooed the dogs away, picked up the ladder, and leaned it against the roof. He stood on the first rung and looked up at her, a cute smile on his face.

"Is okay," he said.

Jessica smiled. She grabbed the ladder, turned around backwards so that she was facing the house, and awkwardly stepped down onto the top rung. Her hands kept a death grip on the sides of the ladder.

Then she realized that this arrangement was giving Ernesto a real eyeful.

"Coming down," she said.

She began to step down the rungs. He stayed anchored with his weight on the bottom rung, so that the ladder didn't slide or skitter.

"Is it okay?" she said.

"It's good," he replied.

She drew closer, her butt mere inches away from his face now. The fieldhand stepped off the last rung and she quickly hopped down onto the ground. She brushed off her clothing.

"*Gracias*, Ernesto," she said.

"You're welcome."

She peered at him. His soft lips were pursed, his dark eyes watching her.

"You speak English, don't you?"

"A little."

"I think more than a little."

He shrugged, his fingers flexing open and closed. "Maybe."

"You don't have an accent."

The fieldhand said nothing.

Jessica shifted her weight. "I'm going to guess something else."

"Okay."

"You want Stanley and Young Billy to think you're dumb. But you're not."

Ernesto turned away. "I need to work."

As she watched him sling the coil of rope around his shoulder and leave, Jessica was absolutely sure that Ernesto was hiding a secret.

And she was going to find out what it was.

Chapter Twenty-Four

AT FIVE A.M. the next morning, a pot of coffee brewing, Jessica laced up her boots. It was her first day of chicken coop responsibilities.

In the kitchen, she whisked together some pancake batter. It came from a box. The night before, Nonna had confessed that she'd been using Bisquick for years, so Jessica didn't feel too guilty about not making the batter from scratch. It didn't seem like one of those items that could be improved upon by being homemade. Sifted flour was sifted flour.

She poured four cakes onto the griddle, flipped them, and slid the finished products onto the plates just as the three men entered the breakfast area. She let the bacon drain on a paper towel, then served it on a large plate. Then, while she got four more pancakes going, she defrosted a bag of frozen berries in a bowl of hot water, drained it, and served it in a bowl mixed with yogurt.

That should be enough.

She sat down at the table. Stanley was eyeing her suspiciously. "This is a real breakfast," he said. "Nice work."

"Thank you." She chewed on a piece of bacon.

"So where's that rain gauge?"

"I didn't buy it."

"Why?"

"Tommy was trying to rip me off."

She explained yesterday's events, the refusal to accept credit cards, the two-hundred-dollar fee to pay cash.

Young Billy shook his head. "He should just sell the store now instead of choking all of us like this."

"I can get equipment and feed cheaper by delivery anyways," said Stanley. "Shoot, we use Hackmore's just because it's close by." He looked at Jessica. "I'll get a rain gauge from our distributor."

"Are you sure?"

"Yep."

"Thank you."

He glanced at her wordlessly. The implication was clear: *Don't mess up again.*

The four of them finished their breakfast. Jessica cleared the plates, dumped them in the sink.

She would clean them later.

Out in the fields, under the first cracks of a cold dawn, Jessica pushed a wheelbarrow filled with two bags of chicken feed over the rutted earth.

Her destination: the four red chicken coops that were parked out in the middle of the field like a circus that had just rolled into town.

Arriving at the destination, she set down the wheelbarrow and caught her breath. The rear doors of all four coops awaited her. Inside would be probably fifteen eggs in each.

She picked up the plastic bucket from the ground, unlatched the first coop, and began reaching inside. The darkness was filled with the moist smell of live poultry. The sound of clucking, squawking, singing. Her fingers scrambled under feathers and straw until they discovered, at last, the thin egg membranes, warm to the touch. It was weirdly thrilling. After all, she'd watched Hitchcock movies. Jessica was alone out here, far from the others, and if these birds decided to gang up on her, she would be finished.

At last, she closed and latched the final coop. She looked down into the bucket. She'd gathered nearly sixty eggs. Young Billy said that her last job was to move the coops, refill the feed, and then carry the eggs back to the outdoor refrigerators alongside the barn.

Jessica looked at the rubber handles. Four heavy coops, eight handles, thirty feet each, one hundred twenty feet total.

She shook her head. There was a better way.

It would involve the tractor.

Jessica placed the bucket of eggs into the wheelbarrow and gently rolled it back across the field to the barn. At the refrigerators, she placed them into the cardboard egg cartons, one by one, and slid the cartons into the cool units.

Then she approached the tractor. Parked near the barn, it was an old model. Jessica still remembered when Nonna had purchased it. At age six, she hadn't been allowed anywhere near it, not even for a fun evening ride, Nonna sternly stating that tractors were not toys. She'd even warned that the tractor was made of butter, and that if Jessica ever touched it, it would melt.

Jessica was still wary of the machine.

She circled the tractor, taking in its contours. Young Billy had mentioned, on the drive from the airport a few days earlier, that tractors were manual shifts. Before her time in New York City, Jessica had been a damn good stick shift driver. It was remarkable since most people her age, even the guys, had grown up on automatic transmission.

The tractor's keys were in the ignition, as she'd expected. No reason to take them out.

Putting the toe of her boot into the tread of the tractor tire, Jessica climbed into the seat. She found the clutch, accelerator, and brake. The shifter was horizontal, six gears, including reverse. It felt just like a car. Jessica smiled. She fastened her seatbelt, put the shifter in neutral, and turned the ignition. The engine didn't turn over—just like a car on cold mornings—so she tried again, giving it a little gas.

Finally the engine rumbled to life. She waited a minute before popping the clutch and slowly sliding into first gear. The tractor pulled forward.

A half-minute later, the cold air biting her nose, Jessica was driving the one-thousand-pound metal vehicle across the grassy field. Even though it felt too slow, she stayed in first gear, because she didn't want to push her luck.

The chicken coops drew closer. She circled around to their front sides, hit the brake, shifted into reverse, and backed up to the first chicken coop. Then she shifted into neutral, threw the brake, and cut the engine.

This tractor was easy.

She undid her seatbelt, hopped off the seat, and hooked up the three-point hitch to the chicken coop's drawbar. She'd seen Nonna hook up the hitch hundreds of times.

She made sure it was secure, then climbed back onto the tractor seat. She started up the engine again, popped the clutch, slid into first, and prepared for a very short five-second ride.

To her surprise, the tractor leaped forward like a bull out of the gate.

Panicking, she was bounced up, nearly off her seat, her right leg nearly flying up over her head, her left foot mercifully hooked under the clutch. It was the only thing saving her. She'd forgotten to put on her seatbelt.

The tractor careened crazily forward over the turf, the chickens clucking in the back. Jessica wrestled her own body down into the bouncing seat. She forced herself to assess the situation.

Then she found the problem.

She'd accidentally gone from a dead start into third gear. Either she was a natural-born tractor driver, or the transmission was extraordinarily smooth, because skipping two gears was hard to do.

It was time to downshift.

Jessica stamped her foot on the clutch, then threw the stick into neutral. To her surprise, nothing changed. The engine continued blatting, the tractor continued its fast crawl, behind her the chickens continued their panicked clucking.

Jessica felt panic eating up her innards. *The tractor was driving ... but it was in neutral.* This broke all the laws of space, time, and internal combustion engines.

The only answer: she must've broken the stick.

Inside her, the panic grew stronger. Ahead, she saw the neat rows of the tilled fields looming larger. Stanley would never forgive her if she drove the tractor straight across the rows, rampaging like a boar, destroying the crops. Desperate, Jessica wrenched the steering wheel to the right. The tractor lurched, her body slid to the left, and behind her the chicken house went up on its left wheel. She heard the soft thuds of chickens falling against the wooden sides of the coop.

A hundred eighty degrees later, the tractor had straightened out, and now Jessica was heading straight back towards where she'd started. The other three coops were growing larger on the horizon. She had about fifteen seconds to figure this out.

But there was nothing to figure out. Jessica was screwed, sitting atop an ungovernable vehicle that she never should've imagined that she could drive.

To her left, at the bottom of a grassy incline, was a small copse of sycamores. She decided to turn for it.

She was going to run the tractor into a tree.

The ground sloped downward, the soil growing looser, the tractor slipping and sliding a bit more. Jessica tightened her hands on the wheel, desperate to maintain, if not the acceleration, then at least the control of the steering. Behind her, the sound of wood and wire shaking, the chickens clucking madly in a chorus of guilt.

At the bottom of the hill, the first tree came into sight—a nice thick sycamore, its branches high enough that Jessica wouldn't blind herself. The trunk was at least three feet across, enough to stop a tractor, if it hit dead on.

That was the question.

The tractor came in hot, third gear feeling faster than it had before, and Jessica didn't see the large rock cloaked in dirt. It hit the outside lip of the tractor's tire, so that the tire slipped to the right, shifting the whole tractor. Bracing for impact, Jessica watched in horror as the grill sailed past the tree. Too late, she turned the wheel left. The sound of bark shredding against wire mesh greeted her ears.

Then Jessica was past the tree—and looking at a ditch that was suddenly yawning in front of her.

There was no time to react. She watched the front of the tractor pitch over the lip. She felt the whole vehicle tilt at a forty-five degree angle and begin to crawl a few feet down—

—and then stop.

She peered down at the tires. Under the thin layer of green was thick, soupy mud. The tires were spinning uselessly.

Jessica twisted around. The chicken coop had sunk a full foot into the muck. The rear wheels were completely submerged. It was stuck.

But the tractor's engine was still in third gear. She could

hear it revving, the RPMs stacking up, the tires spinning hot in the mud. This could end badly. The engine could seize up.

Jessica reached for the key and turned it with all her might into the off position. The engine died. She yanked the key out from the machine and stared at the situation.

It was over, but she'd screwed up.

Badly.

Chapter Twenty-Five

THE SHAPES of the three men appeared at the top of the hill, black silhouettes against the rising orange sun.

Jessica was in the tractor seat, shivering. It had suddenly seemed colder once the excitement had died down. She watched the three men come stumbling down the slope, past the copse of trees, and stop at the edge of the ditch.

"Jay-sus," said Young Billy.

"Hot damn," said Stanley.

Even Ernesto looked shocked.

Jessica looked at them, utter defeat written upon her face. "I made a mistake."

"At first I thought you were taking a joyride," said Stanley.

"We were yelling at you to jump off," added Young Billy.

"I didn't hear you," she replied.

"So let me guess," said Stanley. "You put it into third by accident, right?"

Jessica nodded sadly.

"And then you couldn't get it out?"

She nodded again.

Young Billy shook his head. "This tractor does unpredictable things. See, in that case, you needed to pop the clutch, shift into fifth, and *then* shift down."

"I can't shift down from third?"

"When it's being temperamental, no. Only from fifth."

"I didn't know that."

"If you'd jumped clear of it, it would've stopped automatically. There's a seat sensor. Nonna paid extra for that years ago."

Jessica looked at Stanley. He had grown oddly silent, arms crossed, studying the chicken coop.

"What's wrong?" said Young Billy.

"I think the chickens are dead."

"What?"

Jessica turned. Inside the coop, the chickens were lying on the ground, clawed feet pointed to the sky. It looked like a bloodless massacre.

"Naw, they're just stunned," said Young Billy. "I've seen this happen once when I was a kid, after an earthquake. The chickens didn't talk or move for three days."

"Really."

"Swear on the holy book. They didn't lay eggs for at least a week neither."

"Well, we gotta pull them out. Ernesto?"

The Mexican made some hand gestures, a few mumbled words in Spanish. Stanley seemed to understand him. "Ernesto thinks that we should slide some slats of wood underneath the coop's tires."

"I'll go find some," said Young Billy.

"No," said Stanley, putting a hand on his arm. His eyes were fixed on Jessica. "I think she should do it."

"That's fair," said Young Billy.

Jessica unbuckled her seatbelt and jumped off the tractor. She sank up to her ankles in cold mud.

"I wouldn't trust me to fix anything," she said, "even if this is entirely my fault."

"We'll oversee the repair."

With effort, Jessica slogged her way across the muck and up the side of the ditch. She walked past the three men.

"Your boots are muddy, city girl," said Stanley.

"Yep," she answered.

"Still think you can handle life out here?"

Jessica didn't answer.

Two hours later, after she'd shoved a pair of two-by-fours underneath the tires, after she'd unhooked the three-point hitch from the drawbar, after she'd driven Young Billy's truck up to the edge of the ditch and hooked the winch up to the coop and drawn it manually out of the mud, after her feet had turned into two blocks of frozen mud, after she'd plopped down on a tree trunk and bawled her eyes out—

—Jessica admitted to herself that Stanley maybe, just maybe, had a point.

Maybe she *was* a city girl.

Chapter Twenty-Six

"I DON'T THINK I belong here," said Jessica.

She sat in Nonna's bedroom, curled up in a Queen Anne's chair, a pair of her grandmother's slippers on her feet, a cup of tea resting cozily in her palm. The yellow walls were lit brightly by the morning sunlight pouring through the white lace that covered the windows.

From the chair opposite here came the sound of clacking needles. It was her grandmother, in the matching Queen Anne. It was painful watching her try to learn how to knit with only one functional hand. Jessica watched her gnarled fingers working the needles. It was a typical habit of an elderly woman, and even Nonna admitted knitting wasn't so much practical as it was something to occupy herself. After all, there were only so many potholders, afghans, and sweaters a person could possibly use.

"Don't be silly," said her grandmother. "Of course you do."

"I make so many mistakes. Stanley hates me."

"Stanley doesn't like anybody."

"I almost broke the chicken coop."

"You got it out."

"It took two hours and I cried three times. And now twenty chickens are so stressed out that they won't move."

"That's okay."

"No, it's not. I paralyzed your chickens, Nonna. They're in shock."

Her grandmother chuckled quietly. "The poultry will be fine, dear. And the reason Stanley distrusts you is that he and I are splitting the profits from this farm."

Jessica turned to face her. "Really? When did this start?"

"From the moment I hired him, seven years ago. He didn't want to work at AgriCon, and I needed his science. So, our deal is, after expenses, we split everything fifty-fifty."

"But—"

"It's worked. He sees you as eating into his profits."

It all became clear. Jessica began to understand his hostility. It wasn't personal. It was financial.

"So," said Nonna, "do you think you've learned a lesson today?"

"I've learned not to drive the tractor again."

"The bigger lesson, dummy."

"What?" said Jessica, hearing a note of hysteria rise into her voice. "That I don't have what it takes to make it on the farm? If this were a reality show, I would've been kicked off already."

Nonna lifted her plastic cup of tea with shaking hands. "Goodness, you are certainly down on yourself."

Jessica slouched down in the chair and threw a blanket over her head. "You know who I get it from."

"Yes, I do." The clacking began again as Nonna returned to her needles. Then she said: "By the way, she called this morning."

The old woman's eyes flicked over to her granddaughter.

"Oh?" said Jessica. Her fingers toyed with the fringe on the blanket. Her tone was studiously casual.

Nonna continued: "I told her that you were here. *Why* you were here. How you've left the city. How you're trying to help me." She paused, her eyes flicking up. "I hope you don't mind."

Jessica had fixed her grandmother with an intense but distant stare. "What did she say?"

"She's been thinking about you. She wants to talk to you, whenever you feel like it." Nonna paused. "She also mentioned coming up to visit."

"Here?"

Nonna shrugged. "It's been nearly twenty years."

"I'm surprised she's been able to avoid you this long."

"Your mother has spent her life avoiding me."

"I know."

Nonna sighed. "And now you're doing the same to her."

Jessica fell silent. She'd never thought of it that way.

"She also said," continued Nonna, "that Chase has a few days off in August. She might try to get him to come up too."

Jessica rolled her eyes. Her mother had spent most of her thirties in rehab, in therapy, in psychiatric evaluations, trying to figure out why she was so hopelessly attracted to over-controlling men.

Ten years of this were flushed down the toilet when she found Chase, the most overcontrolling man on the planet. The only positive difference between Chase and his predecessors was that he didn't hit her.

"He's the biggest reason I don't want to talk to her," said Jessica.

"I can't say I disagree with you," said Nonna, "but we all make our own decisions in life."

Easy to say, thought Jessica. But it was hard to respect

other people's decisions when those decisions directly damage your own life.

"I'd prefer not to see him," said Jessica.

"We can talk about it later," answered her grandmother.

Jessica stretched luxuriously and finished her tea. "I guess I'd better get back outside."

"You'd better not," said Nonna. "I insist that you stay right there and keep me company."

"But I need to help—"

"Jessie, they'd probably appreciate it if you just sat out the rest of the day." She smiled reassuringly. "Besides, we haven't talked like this in ages."

Jessica pouted, then stood up. "Fine, I will get more tea. That will be my big chore for the afternoon."

"Very good," said Nonna, laughing. "And when you come back, we can figure out some new ideas that you can suggest to Stanley to make yourself useful around here."

Chapter Twenty-Seven

AS JESSICA TOOK a seat at Chickadee's Saloon, she felt the eyes of the drinkers at the bar watching her.

The men were dressed in jeans and polo shirts and baseball hats, and they were openly staring. People in this area didn't feel any shame in watching strangers, not like in the city, where everyone always looked away from one another.

She was here to meet Mikey. He'd called and asked her out for a beer, to chew over old times, to get reacquainted. It was a sweet gesture, and she'd accepted. She had no expectations from the evening except some nostalgia.

The bartender flipped a cocktail napkin towards her. "What can I get you this evening?"

"A beer."

"What kind?"

"Your choice."

He slid a Michelob towards her. "That'll be three-fifty."

She was about to pull out her wallet when a voice behind her said, "I'll take care of this."

She turned. It was Mikey. He was holding a bouquet of flowers.

Jessica felt her hand quickly cover her heart. "Are these for *me*?"

"No, they're for Ryan." He nodded at the bartender. "Ryan and I go way back. Here you go, honey."

Mikey handed the flowers to the bartender, who accepted them with a grin on his face. "Oh sweetie, I know *just* where to put them."

He pulled out an empty pint glass, filled it with water, and plopped the flowers inside.

"Beautiful," said Mikey.

"Let's just keep them here by the young lady," said Ryan. "She'll make them look more beautiful than we will."

Jessica found herself grinning. "You two should go on the road as a comedy duo," she said.

"Not with him," said the bartender. "Mikey's soybeans would miss him something terrible."

"And those Michelobs won't be serving themselves," said Mikey. He pulled out a stool and perched on the edge of the seat, his palms on the thighs.

"Those flowers were for me, weren't they?" said Jessica.

He clasped his hands to his head, then laid his face down on the counter. "Busted."

"Why?"

He lifted his head. "You don't remember why?"

"No."

"You seriously don't remember why I brought you flowers tonight?"

"No."

He took her hand. "That one summer, I used to pick wild-flowers for you every day."

Jessica scraped her memory. "I really don't remember getting any flowers."

Mikey sighed. "My mother was bent on raising herself a

little George Clooney, so she suggested that I bring you flowers every day. And so every morning I used to pick some weeds from the ditch, throw in some Queen Anne's lace, and lay them on the doormat of your grandmother's house."

"Really?"

He nodded. "My mother always said it had to be done secretly, though."

A secret admirer, thought Jessica. "Well," she said, "I'm sorry to say that I never got them."

"Well, somebody did," he replied.

"My grandmother might've thought I was too young to be getting flowers. Knowing her, she probably threw them to the goats."

"That would explain it," he said.

Ryan was washing dishes at the other end of the bar. "See what chivalry gets you, Mikey?"

"Nothing."

Mikey laughed and drank from his beer. His hand looked comfortable wrapped around the bottle.

"You know what I have to ask next," he said.

"You want to know what I'm doing back here," said Jessica.

"If you're in the witness protection program, better to let me know now."

Jessica heard herself laugh out loud. It sounded strange. She hadn't felt anybody make her belly-laugh in a long time.

His eyebrow lifted diabolically. "Now she's laughing. *Excellent*. Everything is going according to plan."

Still smiling, Jessica said, "What plan is that?"

"It's very dangerous. You shouldn't know."

"Try me."

"Well," he explained, "as you can no doubt see, my stunning good looks and great wealth naturally draw many women to me. But what I find ladies like the most is *funny*. I've got funny working for me."

From the other end of the bar, Ryan said, "Maybe you should pay him more."

"No wonder we were such good friends for that one summer," said Jessica. She noticed that he flinched at the word *friends*. "Well, my story is simple. I am a refugee from New York City."

"Ah," he said, "one of *those*."

Jessica swatted him in the shoulder. "What does *that* mean?"

"Oh, you can figure it out." He winked at Ryan.

"Stop flirting with your boyfriend and look at me. What does *one of those* mean?"

He smirked. "Why don't you explain to me what you were doing there, and I'll let you know."

A pair of beers slid between them. "This one's on me," said Ryan. "For leaving the city."

Jessica found herself explaining, over the next ten minutes, the intricacies of her life in the city—the convicted financier boyfriend, the empty job at the fashion magazine, the horrific cost of living.

When she was finished, Mikey sipped his beer. "I stand corrected," he said. "You are definitely not one of *those*."

"Good to know. What about you?"

His demeanor changed. "Went to college, got hired at AgriCon. Been there four years. Hate it."

"Why?"

He looked at her oddly. "Imagine," he said, "that agriculture was undergoing the biggest change of the century, with more people buying direct from grower, and good organic food too, sustainably farmed—and yet you found yourself on the other side. Instead of David, you were part of Goliath."

"You can always quit," said Jessica.

"No," he replied, growing more animated, "and here's why. I'm going to singlehandedly subvert the industrial farming system. I'm going to change AgriCon from the inside."

"How?"

Ryan said, "He's going to blow up their silos at night."

"Agri-terror," added Mikey. Suddenly he pounded his fist on the bar counter. "What *is* a chicken nugget, Ryan?"

The bartender replied, "I don't know, Mikey. What *is* a chicken nugget?"

They both turned to Jessica and shouted, in unison: "*What is a chicken nugget?*"

This'd been clearly rehearsed. "I don't eat them," she said.

"We don't believe you," said Ryan.

"Well, maybe just one. But I'd have to be real drunk."

Mikey and Ryan exchanged a knowing glance. A shot of whiskey suddenly materialized before her.

"*Stop it*," said Jessica, giggling. "I'm *not* getting drunk tonight. You said we were supposed to talk about old times."

"You barely remember the old times," Mikey replied. "And it was only one summer anyways." His voice took on a bitter tone.

"I remember you used to be skinny."

He paused, looking at her, and too late she realized that the comment had come off more aggressively than she'd expected.

"I'm sorry—"

"No, it's good to be honest. And yes, I *am* turning into a fatass. So thanks for rubbing it in." He patted his gut. "Bet you never saw this in New York. Everybody so sleek and sophisticated."

"Yeah, but a lot of the men are gay."

He shrugged. "You're just trying to make me feel better."

"It's hard to date there for a single girl."

Their conversation went on, and it felt so good that, by the time she stumbled out to her car after midnight, Jessica had begun to wonder why she had ever left the farm to begin with.

Chapter Twenty-Eight

"THE MOST IMPORTANT piece of equipment on any farm," said Stanley, "is its fencing."

It was an hour past dawn, and Jessica was walking with the farm manager across the fields towards the cow pasture. In her hands was a notebook. With some prodding from Nonna, he had consented to giving her granddaughter a tour of the cow pasture. Until now, it'd been off-limits to Jessica. She hadn't minded the oversight. Cows were in some ways the Cadillacs of the farm, the most valuable merchandise on the lot, and you didn't promote the rookie to a starting position.

Jessica was serious about helping the farm succeed, and she was going to prove it to him by taking notes. She also planned to impress him by suggesting some ideas that Nonna had helped her cook up the night before.

"Okay," she said, jotting a note.

"First thing you do every morning," he said, "is check the fences. And cattle get itchy too."

"I'm not scratching any cows."

He didn't laugh. "No, they take care of that themselves,

and fence posts are their favorite scratching posts. So that's why—"

"—we check the fences first thing every morning."

"Exactly," said Stanley. "One loose calf means a half-day of lost work."

"Why?"

"You have to chase it down, rope it, load it. Worst case is you have to call someone for help. Then it gets expensive. The whole problem is just terrible hard."

They approached the gate. Stanley unlocked the system of latches. "So that's why we triple latch here."

"Just like the goats."

He nodded. "You can never have too much protection. Always lock the gate after passing inside."

"Will they try to—"

"Yep," he said, cutting her off, "and cattle are faster than humans. You'll never beat them."

He swung the gate open and gestured for her to enter. She stepped inside the pasture and heard him click the gate shut behind them.

Then Jessica's jaw dropped.

The pasture, for nearly as far as the eye could see, had been rooted up. What had once been, in her childhood, a hard surface of yellow furze had been transformed into loose clumps of rich black loam. On top of the soil was a thick blanket of fresh green growth.

"What did you *do*?" She turned to Stanley. "This field never used to look this healthy."

He puffed his thin chest out. "Thank the pigs. Last fall, they rooted here for about two months. We let it lie fallow over the winter and boom—look what came up last week."

"No artificial fertilizer?"

"None."

She stooped down and plucked a small sprig of green and

lifted it to her nose. It smelled fresh, green, and nutritive. "What is it?"

"White clovers, red-top clover heads, some timothy, a little fescue, you name it."

Stanley began walking along the fence, towards the nearest clump of cattle. They were standing hoof-deep in the rich earth, munching placidly on the new spring growth.

"Now, the cattle. Here's the big picture: Not as annoying as goats, not as smart as the pigs. Oh, and they don't moo."

"I know that," said Jessica. "They *low*."

"And they only do that when they want to leave their pasture."

Behind him, Jessica wrote as fast as she could while walking, her boots tripping over the rich clumps of dirt. "How long will they stay here?"

Stanley swept his arm across the herd. "This is seventy head right now, so they should be good until July. Then we'll move 'em over to Sector B-7."

Sector B-7. Jessica wrote that down. Nonna had used totally different words. Jessica remembered her saying things like *Grandpappy's second apple orchard past the ditch.*

Ahead, a group of seven calves were roughhousing in the field, running in circles around one another. Stanley held a up a warning arm. "These young ones are a little frisky right now, so let's keep our distance and stay by the seat."

"What seat?"

He pointed along the fence. A small wooden seat had been built on top of the second bar.

"Is that in case of emergency?"

Stanley nodded. "That was mostly for when we had the bull. He's gone now, but you never know. Safety is the name of the game here."

They leaned against the fence on either side of the seat. The teenage cattle were dashing in gleeful circles. As they drew closer for a pass, something caught Jessica's eye. She peered closely. On each animal's lower back was some sort of artificial patch.

Stanley noticed her studying them. "You see something?"

"On their backs—"

"That's a heat sensor."

"To check if they're sick?"

He grinned. "To check if they're ovulating."

"What?"

Stanley whipped out his phone. Jessica sidled up to him, happy that he seemed to be warming up to her. His fingers flew across his screen, bringing up a bar graph with a monthly history.

"This," he said, "is an estrous cycle app."

"You're kidding me," said Jessica.

"Nope. The heifers are all patched. This tells me when to call my AI guy."

"AI?"

"Artificial insemination."

"Oh."

"We used to leave everything up to the bull, but he was losing fertility. I decided to give 'em some assistance."

"You could've just bought a new bull. Isn't that cheaper?"

Jessica waited for a response, hoping that it was a good comment.

Stanley ruffled the back of his head. "It depends."

She took a deep breath. "Thinking about it," she said, "just as an outsider, I'm guessing that you have to pay for insurance, and feed, and veterinarian bills, but it's still got to be cheaper than calling an AI guy—"

Truth be told, Jessica felt like a bit of a fraud, trying to talk about farm practices she really could only guess at. She must not have done too bad a job, though, because Stanley held up a hand, quieting her. "There are a lot of variables. Only time will tell."

The farm manager turned and leaned his belly against the fence, propping his elbows sideways on the beam, his jaw working an unseen piece of gum. It was a classic pose, one she'd seen in a thousand movies.

"This doesn't seem too challenging," said Jessica.

"Right now," he answered, "with none of the ladies in heat and everybody out to pasture, there's nothing to do. In a couple months, though, we'll start making hay."

She followed his finger towards a nearby field, where the new hay was already calf-high.

"Nonna never liked making hay," she said.

"That's not true," he said.

"She really doesn't, Stanley. It hurt my grandfather's back so bad that he couldn't walk the last two years of his life."

He regarded her. "Sorry to hear that. But what do *you* know about baling hay?"

Jessica licked her lips, trying not to telegraph her excitement. This was one of the topics that she and Nonna had prepared last night.

"I know that you're losing money by still doing it yourself," she said.

He didn't reply at first. Jessica waited with baited breath. Finally he said, "Go on."

"Nonna told me about all the time you spent fixing that old baler. Greasing it, checking the belts. God, those belts. How many belts have you had to replace?"

"A lot," he admitted, "but I can see where you're going, and here's my response: It's just not a farm without hay baling."

Jessica's eyes flashed. At last, she'd found his weak spot, the chink in his armor. "That's very romantic, Stanley. But it's not practical."

"I don't care."

"Your wallet might."

He was holding very still, eyes on the distant horizon. "Maybe."

"It might be better just to let the cattle graze on all the pastures, all spring and summer long. Then you can buy hay for the winter. It'll save you time, energy, and frustration. It can't be too hard to find someone with excess hay."

"Shoot, lots of folks around here wouldn't mind lightening their loads."

"That's what I mean."

"Problem is," he said, "these cattle are Charolais. I don't know if the breed can handle five straight months of fresh pasture."

"I don't understand."

"Charolais get sick from too much clover."

"Okay," Jessica countered, "then here's what you do. Once every few weeks, corral them in a smaller pasture, a totally defoliated one. You buy a gravity feeder and fill it with some barley or silage or something. Let them feed on that for a day or two."

"But the inspectors—"

"They don't have to know. You loan the gravity feeders to somebody else during the inspections, or maybe just empty them. It can still be marketed as one hundred percent grass-fed beef."

"That would be a lie."

Jessica rolled her eyes. "True, it'll only be ninety-nine percent grass-fed beef. But I round up, and the point is, you need that label to read one hundred percent grass-fed. Believe me. In New York City that's all anybody is talking about. In the wealthier parts of the country, they won't even look at industrially-produced beef anymore."

An astonished look appeared on Stanley's face. "Jessica,"

he said, "where on earth did you get this kind of agricultural sense?"

"Just because I own high heels doesn't mean I'm stupid," she replied.

"Fair enough."

She tucked a hank of hair behind her ear. "So what do you think?"

"Well, that's what I'm gonna do. I'm gonna *think*."

"Okay." Then Jessica hoisted herself up onto the fence seat. "I'll be sitting right here whenever you've finished thinking."

She winked at him. Flummoxed, Stanley mopped his brow and began to walk away, back towards the entrance to the pasture.

He stopped and turned back to Jessica. "Don't—"

"—forget to lock the gate," she finished. "I know."

Chapter Twenty-Nine

THAT WEEKEND, during the hourlong ride to the Raintree Saturday farmers' market, Young Billy shared with Jessica the secret to running a profitable stand at the farmers' market.

"Never wholesale," he said.

"Never?"

"The chefs are always the first to show up. They're going to try to cut a million deals with you. Never do it. Sell direct to consumer only."

"Okay."

He glanced over at her. "That's a nice outfit."

Jessica was dressed in a cute pair of fresh denim overalls. Beneath that, what little cleavage she had was on display in a fresh crew-neck t-shirt. Nonna had approved the outfit. She'd noted that young women are always used to sell products, everywhere, and fresh vegetables at a farmers' market were no different.

Jessica smiled. "Thank you. Should I put my hair into pigtails?"

"That might be pushing it a little too far. You'd look like the girl on the Wendy's sign."

"Good point."

The Saturday farmers' market was held in the parking lot of a shopping mall, a grid of white-topped tents temporarily erected in front of the big-box corporate stores. Pulling into the lot, Young Billy parked the truck along the curb and began unloading the material. Jessica saw that he was beginning to assemble his own white tent at a distant space on the opposite side of the grid from the entrance.

Jessica peered around. "Wouldn't it be better to be closer to the customer parking? We're kind of near the back."

Young Billy locked the final tent arm into place. "They charge more for those spaces. Besides, our regulars will find us anywhere."

Jessica shrugged and assisted him. She unfolded the wooden tables, arranged the zucchini in the box, stood the asparagus on its end, piled the rhubarb high, opened the crates of Swiss chard and spinach. It was an easy setup; Young Billy had practiced the layout in the barn the night before.

While she pulled out the money box, Jessica felt eyes upon her. Across the pedestrian concourse, a hawk-eyed man was studiously observing her. He was standing behind a table bearing an array of white and yellow cheeses. A sign overhead read *Kent Dairy*.

"Who's that?" she asked.

Young Billy looked over. "That's Richard Kent. He's owned that operation for about twenty years. I like the smoked gouda."

"He keeps staring at me."

"Can't imagine why."

When they'd finished, Young Billy handed her the sign that read *Nonna's Farms*. "You may do the honors."

Jessica lifted the sign onto the easel that she'd erected at the front of the tent, then took a few steps back and admired. This was *her* grandmother's business. *Her* grandmother's products. And someday this could even be Jessica's inheritance, presumably. She felt a surge of pride, of tradition, of belonging.

Meanwhile, Young Billy had opened the cash box and was counting its contents. "Two hundred sixteen dollars," he said, recording it onto a clipboard. "It's still early in the season. Let's see if we can fill this with a thousand dollars today."

"Deal."

Jessica stuffed her hands into her coat pockets, feeling the cold on her cheeks, the fresh vegetal scent filling her nose. She felt more alive right now than she ever had in New York.

Soon, the first shoppers began trickling into the market, strolling down the concourse, the canvas recyclable bags slung over their shoulders. The shoppers were as Young Billy had described them—mostly females, middle-aged, and suburban.

"Just be sweet," he said, "and they'll love you."

A heavy man with bleary eyes stumbled in their tent. Jessica noticed that the hair on his hands and forearms had been oddly singed.

His eyes landed on Jessica and gave her the onceover. A greasy smile spread across his face like rancid butter. "And who's this?"

"My name is Jessica," she said.

"This is Nonna's granddaughter," said Young Billy.

"She looks as cute as a baby sheep."

Jessica's first reaction was to tell him to stuff it. Instead, she remembered Young Billy's warning about customer service.

"*Baaa*," she retorted.

The man laughed. "And a comedian too," he said. "You'd better keep this one all for yourself, Young Billy. You're not getting any younger."

Young Billy gave her a sympathetic glance. "What are you looking for today, chef?"

"About twenty pounds of carrots," he said. "I've got some beef bourguignon for the special tonight, and I've got to get it in the oven by noon."

"We've got it," said Young Billy, turning to the truck and hauling out a crate of carrots, the green tops poking over the edge. "Twenty pounds, that'll be fifty dollars."

"Let's call it forty-five."

"Why?"

"Professional courtesy."

Young Billy shook his head. "You put me through this every week."

The sleazy grin appeared on the chef's face. "You can't expect to sell that many carrots to the average consumer in *Raintree*, can you?"

"We sell out most weeks. It'll be fifty dollars."

The chef reluctantly peeled off a few bills and handed them to Jessica. She counted fifty dollars, then nodded to Young Billy, who handed the crate over.

"Don't come to my restaurant looking for any handouts," said the chef. Then he winked at Jessica. She smiled politely and pretended to rearrange cabbages.

When the man had left the tent, Jessica shook his head. "Are all chefs like that?"

"Most of them."

"He was a bully."

"Yep."

Jessica thought about the economics of that last transaction. Young Billy had just saved the farm five dollars. Not much by itself, but multiplied by hundreds, or thousands, of such transactions each year, however, it was enough to make an enormous difference to Nonna's bottom line.

She thought more about the words *direct-to-consumer*.

That really was the answer. In New York City, everyone she met seemed to be an indie musician, an indie designer, an indie writer. That same model was being replicated out here, in rural America, by indie growers.

They grew busier as the morning progressed, and the trickle of customers became a flood. Old people, young people, women, men, children, couples—all poured past their folding tables. Jessica was kept busy reloading the displays from the truck, lifting shopping bags onto the scale, taking cash, making change—all while listening to the same compliments on her outfit, on her personality, on her vegetables. She smiled so hard she felt her cheeks beginning to crack.

Working with customers was oddly difficult. By the end of the morning, her lower back was aching, her arms were sore, and her mouth was parched.

"I need a break," she whispered.

"Make it quick," said Young Billy.

She went behind the truck with a paper cup of water and gulped it, not looking at anything. Then the hair on her neck sprang up.

She turned around. Across the concourse was Richard Kent, the cheesemonger, his eyes boring holes into her. That wasn't a casual gaze. He wanted something from her, but she was pretty sure she knew what it was, and what her answer would be.

Jessica returned to the tent, and by one o'clock pm, the flood of customers had dwindled to a mere trickle. Young Billy removed the sign, folded the easel, and mopped his forehead. "That's all for today."

Jessica counted the cash box. "One thousand two hundred forty dollars."

"Are you sure?"

She counted again. "Yes.

"We cleared a thousand?"

"Yes."

He whistled low. "That's a first. Our best was eight hundred fifty."

"Maybe it was the weather."

"Maybe. Maybe not."

She saw him glance at her overalls. "Seriously?" she said. "You think it was this outfit?"

"I'd lay bets on it."

As Jessica crated the remaining produce, she felt the eyes again. She whirled around.

It was Richard Kent, and this time, he was inside the tent.

"Hi young lady," he said.

"Can I help you?"

He cleared his throat, shifted his weight. He looked profoundly uncomfortable.

"You're Jessica?" he said.

"Yes. Word must get around."

"I'm Richard," he said, "and I hope you don't think I'm being too forward in asking you a question."

Her defense relaxed a little. This didn't sound sexual. "I'll let you know," she said. "Go ahead."

"Do you have experience teaching?" he asked.

That startled her, and she quickly had to rebalance herself. "Teaching? A little. Why?"

He shifted a little, seemingly embarrassed. "See, I don't know Spanish," he said, "and it's been a real problem communicating with my employees."

"I don't know much Spanish."

"No," he explained, "I'm looking for someone to teach them English."

Jessica cocked her head. "Why don't you teach them?"

"Hell, they won't listen to me. I'm their boss."

"I wouldn't really know where to begin—"

"It doesn't matter." He glanced at her outfit. "They will listen to every word you say."

At last Jessica understood. She was the closest thing to eye candy around here. "Okay," she said, "tell me more."

Richard Kent stuffed his hands into his pockets and looked down, pulling his lips tightly into his mouth. "I can pay you forty dollars for a two-hour lesson."

"Where?"

"On my property. We can schedule it in the evening."

"Where's your property?"

Young Billy interrupted. "Old Crow Road. Maybe fifteen miles down from our place."

"It's not too far," said Richard.

"How many people would I be teaching?" said Jessica.

"I have four workers. All from Mexico. Very nice guys. There won't be any problems."

Jessica mulled the offer, trying to find a downside. There didn't seem to be one. She looked at Young Billy, who was deconstructing a table. He shrugged as if to say *why not*.

"Okay, I guess so," she said.

"Great," said Richard Kent, clapping his hands together. "Let's plan on Tuesday night? At eight pm?"

"That's all right."

"I'll have some materials printed out for you."

"That'll be helpful," she said. "Thank you."

"No, thank *you*."

They shook hands, and as Richard Kent crossed back to his table of cheeses, she found herself wondering down what strange avenues this rural adventure would lead her.

Chapter Thirty

FACING THE COOP, Jessica flexed her hands inside a pair of heavy work gloves and prepared to lift.

On the ground beside her was a bucket of fifteen fresh eggs, which she'd just collected from the hatch in the back. Jessica was relieved that the chickens had recovered from their wild tractor ride. She hadn't wanted to live with the burden of having paralyzed poultry.

Now it was time to move the coop. Young Billy had offered to help, but she turned him down. She was going to do this on her own, with her own arms.

She wiggled her toes inside work boots, took a deep breath, gripped the rubber handles, and lifted the coop. Her triceps straining, Jessica began pulling the contraption across the grass. Her body was tense, straining with the effort.

A few seconds later and thirty feet away, she dropped the handles. The structure crashed to the grass. She turned and watched. Inside the coop, the chickens hopped out of their enclosure and began pecking at the grass.

Jessica stared at the birds, dazed, a stupid grin on her

mouth. She'd done it. She'd lifted a two-hundred-pound coop and dragged it thirty feet across uneven grass.

Farm life was starting to make sense.

She went to the second coop, collected the eggs, getting pecked in the wrists a few times. She understood where the word *peckish* came from and made a mental note about which chickens to avoid. Then she donned the work gloves again and moved the second coop next to the first. She repeated the process with the third and the fourth coops.

When Jessica had finished a half-hour later, she stood back, hands on hips, and surveyed her work.

Tending the chickens was a regular farm chore, and she, Jessica, a girl who'd spent the last year and a half opening boxes of unrequested high heels shoes in a basement office in New York City, was doing it. With no help.

A distant, odd sound from her pocket brought Jessica back into the present. It took a moment for her to realize that it was her own phone. It had sounded unfamiliar to her ears out here, in this field. It hadn't even rung for at least a week.

She looked at the screen. It read *Phineas*.

"Oh my God," she said, then picked up. "What took you so long to call?"

"I thought you'd be back in New York by now," came the voice of her city friend. It zipped her straight back to her old life. "I had to cancel the welcome back party."

"I've been very busy," she replied.

"Milking cows?"

"It's not a dairy farm, Phineas. Vegetables and meat."

"How caveman. Well, I'm looking forward to having a tour."

"You're coming out to visit me?"

"Of course," he replied. "I won't let you wear smelly denims the rest of your life."

"I would love that." She hopped up and down a little. "When do you want to come?"

"I'll be there in about two hours."

Jessica stopped, her eyes looking at a tuft of daffodils. "For real?"

"Yes, for real. I just landed."

"Why didn't you tell me you bought a plane ticket?"

"Well, I *am* telling you." His voice grew more serious. "It was a last-minute thing."

"Let me guess," said Jessica.

"No—"

"I'm going to anyways."

"Please don't—"

"Grande Mast fired you."

There was no answer. "I'm right," Jessica said, "aren't I?"

He sighed. "Yes, you're right."

"I *knew* it. So now you're on an impromptu vacation."

He chortled out loud. "Mayberry or bust. Put the hot water on, Ma Kettle, the party has arrived. When are you picking us up?"

"From the airport?"

"Yes."

Jessica laughed. "I'm not. You can rent a car."

"Girl, I do *not* have that kind of money. I just blew all my savings on this plane ticket."

Jessica shook her head, smiling. Part of Phineas presumed that the whole world would cater to him.

Then she paused. "Wait a minute. Did you just say *us?*"

There was a guilty silence. "I brought some friends."

Jessica grappled for words. "You brought ... *friends.*"

"Yes."

"Do I know them?"

He giggled. "Um, no. Jesus, *I* barely know them."

"Well," said Jessica, "I have a lot to do this morning. I can make it by five pm if I cut out early."

She could hear Phineas pouting. "What are we supposed to do waiting around *here*?"

"Learn to entertain yourself."

"You're such a bitch."

"Is that still a term of endearment?"

"Not today."

"I'll see you at five."

Jessica ended the call and looked at the phone. Normally, a conversation with Phineas lifted her spirits. This time, however, as she began to trudge back towards the farmhouse, she felt an odd sense of dread.

Chapter Thirty-One

THE NEXT MORNING, Phineas strolled into Nonna's kitchen wearing a blue denim cowboy shirt with embroidered roses sewn across the chest. Down each sleeve was a double row of sequins. His pants were denim jeans with flared bottoms. On his feet were a pair of vintage orange cowboy boots that looked like they'd never left cement.

And on his head was perched a white suede cowboy hat.

Jessica was sitting alone at the breakfast table with a mug of coffee. The others had headed out to the fields long ago. Last night, she and Phineas had shared the attic, him sleeping on a pile of blankets on the floor. His friends had taken the spare bedroom.

"Nobody wears those here," she said, peering at his headwear.

"Somebody must."

"No," she said, "it's all baseball caps."

He grimaced. "That is going to change."

"You can try, but people don't like to change here. Women are still dressing in A-line dresses."

"Those were *so* in last fall."

149

"They've never gone out here."

Phineas pulled a handkerchief out of his breast pocket and polished the toe of his boot. "So let's stop ruining my make-believe and have some fun. What is there to do on this property?"

"Usually we start with breakfast."

"No breakfast for me," he said. "I cannot eat anything in the morning."

She smiled quietly. She remembered feeling the same way a few weeks earlier. It was funny how farm living changed that.

She carried her plates to the kitchen, washed them in the sink, then laid them in the rack to dry. Phineas watched her. "Such a domestic goddess," he said. "*Trés* chic."

Jessica turned off the water and hung up the towel. "Doing dishes is stylish?"

"Oh my God, *yes*. There was a dishwashing party in the Hamptons last summer. The millionaires' wives all wore French maids' outfits with yellow rubber gloves. They washed dishes while the help sat outside under the umbrellas and drank cocktails."

"It sounds like a great party," she said.

"Don't be sarcastic."

"Sorry, but I'm not Marie Antoinette. When are your friends going to wake up?"

Phineas craned his neck, peering into the hallway. "There they are. Good morning, sunshines."

Into the kitchen staggered his two hangers-on. One was a tall, skinny man dressed in purple skinny pants, a skinny collared shirt, and a skinny black tie. He looked like he'd just teleported out of 1965 mod London. Last night, he'd introduced himself as Bailey. His handshake had been limp.

The other was a bear of a man, tubby, bearded, and hairy. He'd chosen to wear a tight green t-shirt, a pair of black track pants, new white sneakers, and a gold bracelet. He looked like a refugee from a Long Island deli. He'd introduced himself as Anthony. His handshake had been sweaty.

"Coffee?" she said brightly. It was customary to welcome visitors.

"I'll take a cappuccino," said Anthony.

"We only have drip."

He scowled. "Eww."

"So how do you guys know Phineas?" she asked.

The two hangers-on exchanged alarmed looks. "Ah, well, we don't really know him—"

"We just met Phineas," said Anthony. "Last weekend."

Jessica looked at her friend. "And you invited them to come to my family's farm?"

Phineas smiled weakly. "Come on, I know you're cool with having friends over."

"Yes, *I* am," said Jessica, "but Nonna is recovering from a stroke. And it's her property."

"We'll make nice with grandma," said Anthony. "Bailey can give her a fashion consultation."

"She wouldn't want one," said Jessica.

"She couldn't afford me anyways," sniffed Bailey. "So, Jessica, is there anything *fun* to do out here?"

"Depends on what you call fun."

"Molly and a hot farmboy."

Jessica remembered that *Molly* had been a gay term for Ecstasy, a nightclub drug. "None of that," she answered evenly, "but we do have vegetables, and cows, and goats."

"Goats?" said Anthony.

Jessica stood up. "Let's take a little tour, boys."

She led them outside. The bright sun warmed their shoulders. Anthony donned a garish pair of sunglasses with red frames. Bailey wrinkled his nose.

"Jesus, it stinks," he said.

"It's just drying manure," said Jessica.

"That's disgusting."

"I think it smells sweet," she replied, "and besides, you get used to it."

Phineas minced around a dried patch of mud. "Jesus, it's so *dirty* here."

"That's what farming is," she answered. "Pushing around dirt. Watering it."

"Jesus," he said again, wiping his boots.

Jessica led the three New York boys through the property, across the fields, past the chicken coops, over to the cow pasture. They walked slightly behind her, bitching, teasing, gossiping, doing anything, she noticed, except absorbing the scenery around them.

"Can't we do something *fun*," said Bailey.

"Like what?" said Anthony.

"Like a tractor ride."

"Oh my gosh, yes—"

"Jessica, can you give us a tractor ride?"

"*Pleeease*?"

Jessica smiled, thinking about the truly wild tractor ride she'd taken with the chicken coop. "This is a working farm," she said, "and I think that Stanley was going to be using the tractor this afternoon."

"You are no fun at all," said Phineas.

Then Jessica had an idea.

"You know what?" she said. "Young Billy and I are transferring plug trays from the greenhouse into the fields today. Maybe you could help."

Bailey scoffed. "What did she just say?"

"I thought she said we could work."

"Seriously?"

Jessica bit her lip, willing herself to remain patient. "What I'm saying is that you could pitch in. Get a taste of what real farm life is like."

She led them over to the greenhouse, noticing that the three boys had fallen oddly silent. Inside, Young Billy was arranging the long rows of plug trays into tidy rows. Each had a tiny sprouting head of lettuce.

"We've got some helpers," said Jessica.

Young Billy whooped. "Just what I was hoping to hear. You all can start by transporting those trays outside to the cart."

"Which cart?"

"The one attached to the tractor."

Jessica lifted a tray of baby lettuce heads. It weighed probably twenty pounds.

"Is it heavy?" said Bailey.

"Not really. You can pick it up."

Phineas drew a fingertip along the outside edge. "It's really dirty."

"That's because it's a tray of dirt," said Anthony.

"But it's spilling over the edge."

At last, the three city dwellers managed to lift one tray of lettuce and carry it outside. They shoved it into the shelf of the cart.

"Now what?" said Phineas.

"Now," said Young Billy, hopping onto the tractor, "I drive them out to the field and we plant them."

"Sorry," said Phineas, "I didn't bring the right shoes."

Young Billy looked at Bailey. "What about you?"

"My doctor says I can't do any manual labor. It's a heart condition."

He turned to Anthony. "We could really use an extra hand."

"I want to see the goats," the tubby man answered.

"Shut up about the goats," said Bailey. "God, this place is *boring*."

Jessica shot a disapproving glance at Phineas, who looked

sheepish. She could tell that he was regretting having brought his new city friends.

"I know what you guys could do," said Young Billy. "You could go on a picnic."

"Really," said Anthony. He sounded skeptical.

"Sure. Jessica can help you pack one. We have an old-fashioned basket, a red checkered tablecloth, food."

"Do you have wine?" said Bailey.

"I think so."

"A chaise lounge?"

"You can look out by the creek."

The skinny city boy clapped his hands together. "*Now* it's getting fun. Laying on a chaise lounge under a tree, drinking chardonnay, ponies prancing—"

"I want to see the goats," said Anthony.

"Shut up," said Bailey.

As Jessica led the city people back towards the farmhouse to prepare their picnic, she gave thanks for Young Billy's idea. This would buy her at least three hours of peace.

Chapter Thirty-Two

HAVING SENT the three boys on their way with two bottles of wine and a homemade lunch of salami, cheese, and olives, Jessica didn't see her guests from the city for the rest of the afternoon. She was busy anyways, helping Young Billy transfer the plug trays out of the greenhouse and into the fields.

It was tedious work, digging a small hole with the spade, crouching in the dirt, dropping the tiny plant into the hole, then covering the root system. At the end of each row, she and Young Billy sprayed some water from a hose.

By six o'clock, the sun had begun dropping, and they headed back to the farmhouse, where Jessica washed up, changed jeans, and strapped on a pair of low heels.

When she came downstairs from the attic, Nonna shouted at her from the bedroom.

"I remember that sound," said Nonna.

"Did my mother used to wear heels?" answered Jessica.

"Heavens, no, she was a flower child. I was talking about myself."

Jessica walked into her grandmother's bedroom. The old woman was still in bed, looking a little healthier than she had been a couple of weeks back. Her speech had improved. In her good hand was a Sudoku puzzle.

"Don't you look nice. Are you going on a date?"

"No, I'm going to teach English to migrant workers."

Astonished, her grandmother took off her spectacles. "Really? For who?"

"Richard Kent."

She nodded. "He's always complained about Spanish. Why did he ask you?"

Jessica shrugged. "I figured why not."

"So how are the city slickers doing?"

"I haven't seen them all day."

"Well, I've heard them. They're running around drunker than a bunch of skunks, whooping and hollering." Nonna sighed. "I'm glad you're not with those people anymore."

Jessica looked down at her feet. She was filled with conflicting emotions.

"One more thing," said Nonna. "I have to talk to you after you get back."

Jessica's antenna extended. "About what?"

"It's nothing very important."

"Well, if my friends come back to the house, tell them to call me about dinner."

Nonna smiled. "Oh, they'll be passed out by eight o'clock."

"You're probably right."

Jessica drove down the two-lane blacktop, turned left onto Old Crow Road, and immediately saw a sign for Richard

Kent's dairy farm. She would make this a quick lesson. After all, she didn't really know what she was doing anyways, and had essentially been hired for her moderate sex appeal.

But her mind was on Phineas. She'd felt so close to him back in New York City; now, something had changed. He seemed so prissy, so brittle, so unable to adjust to his new environment. He was like a fragile plant that could only thrive in a very narrow range of temperatures.

Had he always been that way? Or was it that she just hadn't been able to see it in New York?

Then it dawned on her: Phineas hadn't changed at all. He couldn't be anything but himself.

The truth was that *Jessica* had changed.

She stuffed that thought way down into her soul and she turned into the dairy farm and drove up the dirt road. An aluminum fence on either side of the road was anchored into a small berm. From the spaces between the fence slats poked the thick black-and-white heads of at least two hundred Holstein cows, like a row of parade goers.

At the center of the property was the feedlot, a zone of brown dirt nearly the size of a football field with piles of green forage heaped in neat rows. In the middle of the site, beneath a long-shaded awning, were twin rows of milking stalls. Next to the feedlot was a pasture displaying the spring browns.

Another warehouse, this one smaller and more traditional, lay off to the side. Several trucks were parked along it, and a silver tanker had been backed up into its concrete innards. Jessica guessed that was the creamery. She whistled softly through her teeth. Richard Kent had a sizable operation.

She parked the truck next to the others, and Richard came out of the creamery to greet her, wiping his hands on his jeans. "So glad you've made it," he said, shaking her hand.

"My pleasure," said Jessica.

"So you'll be in our conference room over here. There's a whiteboard and some dry erase markers."

"Okay."

He nodded towards a side door in the creamery. "Don't worry, it's not refrigerated. And one more thing."

"What's that?"

"There's going to be a few more people than anticipated."

Jessica furrowed her brow. "Why?"

"Well," Richard Kent explained, "word got out that you would be giving English lessons. And so, I don't know really— they all just kinda showed up here this evening. I guess you're real popular."

"How many are there?"

Richard Kent opened the door to the conference room. Jessica gasped.

Nearly thirty Mexicans had assembled themselves in a room designed to hold less than half that many. They were crammed shoulder-to-shoulder around three round tables, some grinning, some nervous, some silent, others chatting in Spanish in low voices. Their brown fingers drummed orange pencils on the table.

"Is this going to be a problem?" said Richard.

Jessica struggled to find a suitable reply.

"No," she said, "no problem at all. Can I see the materials?"

He grinned sheepishly. "Well, our printer ran out of ink, so you'll have to do this one on your own. I'll replace the cartridge by next week."

Jessica had taught exactly two weeks of English as a Second Language, and that had been over two years ago. She ransacked her memory for any tricks that she could use.

Then she remembered one.

Back to the Board.

"*Hola, clase,*" she said. "My name is Jessica from Nonna's Farm. Richard Kent has graciously paid for this class to happen. How many of you understand what I am saying right now? Raise your hands."

She didn't raise her hand, so that there was no visual cue. Only five out of thirty hands lifted. Jessica scanned those five faces, trying to memorize who to call on in the future for right answers.

Then she saw him—the high mestizo cheekbones, the soft lips, the dark, intelligent eyes—and her breath caught in her throat.

Ernesto.

He was sitting in the back, as calm and imperturbable as a sphinx. Her grandmother's own farmhand, in her class. Why hadn't he said anything to her about wanting to learn more English? Was he too shy? Too frightened? They could've at least shared a ride.

Jessica forced herself to focus on the task at hand. Her eyes swept the class. "I need a volunteer."

She pointed at a guy in a red flannel shirt sitting up front.

"You. Stand up."

He rose, smoothing his shirt. His classmates threw a few insults in Spanish at him.

"Come over here," she said, gesturing. He swaggered over to the dry erase board. "Now stand with your back to the board."

He didn't move. Jessica saw that he hadn't understood, so she grabbed his shoulders and turned him around so his back was facing the board and his front was facing the class.

"Like this."

Now his classmates were laughing at the sight of him being manhandled. She glanced quickly at Ernesto. The tiniest hint of a smile appeared on his impassive face.

"What is your name?"

His eyebrows lifted. "*Como*?"

"What ... is ... your ... name?"

His eyes lit up. "I ... am Ricardo."

"I see," said Jessica, "just like the boss."

His chest literally puffed up and a cocky smile appeared on his face. "*El jefe*."

Jessica turned to the board, opened a dry-erase marker, and wrote the word *cattle*. Then she thought for a moment, and turned back to the class.

"*Describe ese palabra, pero no puede decirlo*." Then she added: "*En ingles, por favor*."

Ricardo tried to turn to see the word. Jessica grabbed his head and forced him to look straight ahead. "No looking. Listen only."

Then she looked at the class. "Speak to him in English. Describe it."

One lifted his hand. "Ees an animal."

"*Animale*?" said Ricardo.

"English only," said Jessica.

"Eet has four toes," said another.

"Not four toes," said another. "Eet has four *feet*. Eet eats the green."

Ricardo scrunched up his forehead. "Eats the green?"

"Grass," said another voice, this one nearly unaccented. "It lives in the pasture and eats lots of grass. When we kill them, we have beef."

Jessica didn't even have to look to identify that voice. It was Ernesto—and his syntax was excellent. The other students turned and looked at him in surprise.

"Thank you, Ernesto," she said. "Ricardo, what word is written on the board behind you?"

A sly smile came over Ricardo's face. "Cow."

The class oohed. "Plural," said someone.

Ricardo thought hard. "Cows?"

Big laughs. They kept him guessing until he finally said, "Cattle." The class erupted in applause. Ricardo pumped his arms in the air and swaggered back to his seat.

"Who wants to go next?" said Jessica.

Every hand in the class shot up.

Chapter Thirty-Three

THE LAND WAS CLOAKED in darkness by the time Jessica stepped out of the creamery. From the blackened fields came the occasional disembodied lowing of an unhappy cow.

Richard Kent was waiting outside the door, his keys in hand.

"Thank you, young lady," he said.

"You're welcome," Jessica replied.

He locked the door behind her. "Can we keep this Tuesday night for the next month?"

She shrugged. "It's fine by me."

"Great."

Jessica barely noticed as he pressed the money into her palm. Then she noticed a lone figure sitting underneath a nearby lamp, his face buried deep in a book.

Ernesto.

"See you next week," said Richard Kent.

"See you then."

Jessica felt herself being pulled across the dirt yard towards the lone figure. As she entered the circle of light, Ernesto looked up, saw her, and quickly stowed the book into his backpack.

"Did you need a ride home?"

His full mouth twitched a little. "My friend's car was full. He is coming back to drive me."

"You can come with me."

That made a lot more sense. Ernesto shrugged, stood up, and slung his bag over his shoulder. He followed her into the Nonna's Farms truck.

On the road back, the silence in the car was palpable. She felt as though Ernesto was daring her to start a conversation. Jessica wasn't going to allow his reticence to dictate their entire relationship.

"Where do you come from, Ernesto?"

"Mexico."

"Which part?"

"Baja."

"Ah," she said, "the home of fish tacos."

She sensed him looking at her. "You've been there?"

"No, but I know fish tacos."

He wiped his face, as though shucking away all his stress. "It's a beautiful place, but it's not a good place for someone who wants a different future."

"You sound like an ambitious person."

The farmhand replied evenly, "I want to improve myself."

"You've certainly improved your English."

"Thank you."

"Did you get it from reading that big book in your backpack?"

"No," he said.

"What's the book?"

"I'm studying."

"For what?"

"Do you really want to know?"

She heard the passion in his voice. Jessica sensed that she was standing at the precipice of something much bigger.

"Yes," she replied.

Ernesto punched the overhead light in the car. Then he reached into his bag and produced the book. He angled the cover so that she could read it.

The Basics of Microbiology. 4th edition.

Jessica glanced at the farmhand. His eyes were boring deeply into her own.

"Are you reading that just for *fun*?" she said.

"Of course not," he replied, "it's very difficult to understand. But I want to be ready for my first college course."

Jessica nearly had to pick up her jaw from the floor of the cab. "I didn't know you were going to *college*."

"Someday," he said.

"Where do you want to go?"

"I think starting at a community college would be the cheapest way. Then I can transfer to a four-year university to finish my degree."

"And then?" said Jessica.

"Then I'm going to veterinary school."

Jessica was astounded. "You've been keeping all this secret from Stanley and Young Billy?"

He didn't respond.

"They think you're stupid because you don't speak to them. They think you don't even know English."

Ernesto sighed. "I let them think like that. It's easier this way."

"But they could help you. Stanley could show you a lot."

His voice grew tight. "Stanley fired the last Mexican for being too smart."

"Really?"

He nodded. "Ask him about Roberto."

"So that's why you came to this class tonight," said Jessica. "It's a cover story."

"So I look just like any other wetback."

Jessica winced at hearing him use the denigration. "I wish you would've told me this earlier," she said.

"Please keep it a secret," he said.

"Just between us?"

"Yes."

"Okay."

His hand grasped her hand. "Do you promise?"

"I promise."

For a moment, they looked into one another's eyes, and he seemed to relax.

As she turned the truck into Nonna's Farms, and began the drive up the long dirt road towards the farmhouse, the truck's headlights swept across the fields.

Suddenly Ernesto bolted up in his seat. "What was that?"

"What?"

He twisted around, looking backwards. "I thought I saw a goat."

"In the field?"

"Yes."

"That's impossible."

They arrived at the farmhouse. As Jessica parked the truck, the headlights raked across the goat enclosure. Ernesto pointed. "Oh no."

"What?"

"Turn left a little. So we can see."

Jessica cranked the wheel. The headlights landed upon the gate to the goat enclosure.

It was open.

Chapter Thirty-Four

"*SHIT*," said Jessica.

"Turn the engine off," said Ernesto, "but keep the head-lights on."

"Okay."

They bolted out of the truck. Ernesto ran to the shed, found a large flashlight, and joined Jessica running across the dirt lot towards the goat enclosure.

Jessica was wearing her heels, so she stopped just before the gate. It was horrifically muddy and shitty inside. Ernesto, who was still wearing his work boots, plunged inside.

"How many are left?" she said.

He turned on the light and swept the enclosure with the beam. "None. They're all out."

Jessica swore under her breath. Twelve goats, running rampant across the farm. From the warning that Young Billy had given her, this was a worst-case scenario. There was no end to the destruction they could cause before the sun rose.

Ernesto reappeared. "Who did this?"

"Guess," she said.

The front door of the farmhouse creaked opened. Jessica

turned around. Phineas had staggered out onto the porch in a burgundy velvet robe, a small glass of green liquid dangling from his hand.

"Thank God you're back," he said. "I've learned two things. One, knitted afghans absolutely slay. Two, we're nearly out of absinthe."

"Phineas—"

He lifted the glass. "Also, Bailey is *obsessed* with your cribbage board. He wants to start a line of handbags based on the notch pattern."

"Answer one question, Phineas. Did you and your friends go into the goat enclosure?"

He froze. "Um, maybe?"

"I specifically told you not to."

"Anthony really wanted to see the goats."

"Well, you didn't lock it when you left."

His brow furrowed, Phineas peered at the gate. "That's weird. We locked it. That latch on the side."

"There are three locks."

"So?"

"One isn't enough. Goats can figure out single locks. And now they're out."

He blanched. "Oh my god, they are *smart* little brats, aren't they? It's no big deal, we'll find them in the morning. As long as we don't wake up too early—"

Jessica's temper broke. "No, we can't wait until morning, Phineas. Goats aren't like cows or sheep. They're *very* destructive. We have to—"

She was cut off by the sound of hoofs on metal, followed by a long, nasally bray. Ernesto swung his heavy flashlight around.

A goat had climbed onto the truck, its hoofs leaving enormous dents in the roof of the cab. It brayed again, tauntingly.

"Oh my God," screamed Jessica. She kicked off her heels and ran in bare feet across the dirt, towards the vehicle.

Ernesto beat her to it. He jumped into the bed of the truck and, without missing a single step, threw himself onto the back of the goat. It took off like a shot down the front of the vehicle, down the hood, Ernesto still clinging to its side.

Jessica watched the goat's back left hoof land hard on the windshield. Then she heard a sickening crunch.

The windshield had shattered. A spiderweb of cracks was emanating from a hoof-sized hole punched in the middle of the laminated safety glass.

The goat leapt off the hood, landed on the ground—

—and was immediately pulled down to the dirt, onto its side, by Ernesto. The Mexican farmhand held the animal in what looked like a wrestling hold, his legs scrabbling for leverage in the dirt. The goat was twisting and writhing and making terrible sounds.

"Jessica, get some rope," he shouted. "Hurry!"

She leaned into the truck bed, picked up the flashlight, dashed into the nearby shed, and swung the beam around until she found a length of rope. She quickly brought it outside.

Handing it to Ernesto, she watched him wind the rope around the animal's neck, make a series of loops, and then throw one end to her. "Take it and *hold on*."

Jessica picked up the rope. She saw Ernesto wind one end around his forearm, so she did the same. Then he released his hold on the goat and quickly rolled out of the way.

The animal leaped to its feet and took off like a shot.

Horrified, Jessica watched the rope play out in her hands. She braced her legs in the dirt and prepared for the worst rope burn of her life.

The reality was even worse. Jessica weighed one hundred

and ten pounds soaking wet, and as the rope went taut, she was yanked clean off her feet.

In the blink of an eye, she found herself being dragged on her belly across the dirt by a rampaging goat. In her good outfit, no less.

Nearby, Ernesto had planted his feet wide apart, leaning back slightly, his biceps bulging with the effort of controlling the animal. Still, he was being dragged too, though not as dramatically.

"Let go," he shouted. "You'll get hurt otherwise."

Jessica managed to unwind her arm from the rope and roll away. She watched it slide away from her.

"Stand up," said Ernesto, "and try again."

Jessica picked herself up, grabbed the rope again, braced herself, and pulled hard.

With serious pressure from two opposite directions on its neck, the goat was finally stopped in its tracks. She could sense its breathing, its power.

"Now," said Ernesto, "walk the animal back into the gate. Keep your arms strong."

The goat pranced and bucked, but their combined strength, pulling tightly, kept the animal in place. In this way, they slowly maneuvered the goat back into its enclosure. Once inside, Ernesto slipped the rope off the animal's neck, then ran out quickly. Jessica shut the gate behind him and locked all three latches.

They both stood there, breathing hard.

"Now I understand," she gasped, "why Young Billy calls *goat* a four-letter word."

Ernesto brushed off his shirt. "And only eleven more to go."

"I think I need to change first," she answered, looking at her ruined blouse.

On the porch, Phineas was watching them, an expression of pure shock on his face.

Chapter Thirty-Five

AT A LITTLE AFTER nine o'clock am, as Ernesto closed and triple-locked the gate to the goat enclosure for the twelfth and final time, Jessica slumped against the fence, exhausted.

They'd worked through the entire night, running across the fields, capturing errant goats, roping them, wrestling them. As the sun had appeared on the horizon and risen into the sky, Jessica had gotten a better sense of the destruction.

It'd been worse than she'd imagined. A decorative fence surrounding the tomato plants had been knocked down, and the plants eaten down to the nubs. Four rows of baby lettuce and five rows of spring onions had been completely decimated. All of Nonna's rose bushes had been stripped clean. One goat had even gotten inside an unlocked supply closet near the cow pasture and had wreaked havoc, scattering tools for fifty feet in every direction.

Capturing a rogue goat was a delicate art, she'd learned. First, she'd used a bucket of grain to lure each animal to a position alongside the nearest strong fence. As it arrived to feed, Ernesto had forcefully pinned the animal against the fence with his knee, while Jessica had quickly tethered it with a chain. Then Ernesto had wrestled it to the ground and trundled its four hooves together using plasticuffs. Lastly, the two of them dragged the animal, which was usually bleating madly by this point, into the back of the truck for a drive back to the enclosure.

They had performed this eleven times. After a while, Jessica didn't notice the sweating, the stinking, the thrashing, the bleating. This had become another day at the office.

Now, sitting next to her against the fence, swigging from a water bottle, Ernesto looked at her admiringly. "You surprise me, Jessica," he said.

"Oh yeah?" she said.

"When you first arrived, I think to myself, 'She will stay one week, maximum.' I think that you're too used to the city."

Jessica wiped her face on a rag. "I spent time here as a little girl."

"I can tell. You did a good job."

He held out a sweaty hand. She grasped it. The handshake lingered longer than usual.

"Now," he said, "what are you going to do about your friends?"

"We're going to have a conversation."

She dragged herself to her feet and walked back to the farmhouse, feeling the effects of an entire night spent running, jumping, tethering, dragging, and driving eleven large mammals. Every fiber of every muscle in her body ached.

On the front porch of the farmhouse, Phineas was sitting in a rocking chair. He was wearing a white bathrobe and had a glass of freshly squeezed orange juice.

"Howdy," he said. "You look like something the goat dragged in."

"Phineas, I spent all night hunting them down. They ruined parts of this property. And it was your fault."

"The perils of absinthe," he said. "The green fairy strikes

again. There's nothing a fairy hates more than being chased by other fairies."

It was an elaborate joke, and he waited for a laugh, the way Jessica had at their desks, in the old days.

"We're not at *Spretza* anymore," she replied. "We're at my grandmother's farm."

"True."

"And what you did last night was ... totally disrespectful."

He sighed. "I know, but we were just having so much fun, and Anthony was so insistent that we meet the goats."

"They ate a bunch of crops, Phineas. You saw the one break our windshield. That's probably going to cost us five hundred dollars—all because of you and your friends."

Phineas' face grew downcast. "I'm sorry."

"You should be."

"What do you want us to do?"

Jessica drew a deep breath. Her lips didn't want to form the next words. "The three of you probably need to leave."

Phineas looked confused, as though this were impossible. "But we just *got* here."

"Nonna isn't going to let you stay," she replied, "not once she hears about this. It would be better if you left on your own first. And paid for some of the damages."

Her friend fixed her with a stare. "What do *you* want me to do?"

As Jessica prepared to answer, she felt a pain like a knife ripping into her heart. "I want you to leave, Phineas. I'm sorry. You guys just don't fit on a farm."

He stood up, a hurt expression on his face.

"I really wish this could be different."

"I understand," he said, standing up. "We invited ourselves, we fucked up your farm, and now you want us out. It makes perfect sense. We are city people, not fashion-challenged, flyover-state fuddy-duddies in mom jeans and ugly bobs. It was a mistake to think that you could ever like us."

"That's not what I'm saying—"

"It's fine, Jessica, it's really fine."

The door swung open, and Bailey and Anthony stepped outside. Phineas placed one hand on each of their chests and pushed them back inside. "Pack up, we're leaving."

"But—"

"Don't ask any questions. We have to go."

As they retreated back into the house, their babbling voices fading away, Jessica dropped her head and leaned against the porch railing, feeling part of herself fading away as well.

Chapter Thirty-Six

AS YOUNG BILLY came limping across the dirt yard, his face was wincing in serious pain.

Jessica looked up from the repurposed tub that she was rinsing out. "What's wrong?"

It'd been two weeks since Phineas and company had departed, and Jessica had found herself swept up in the rush of springtime chores on the farm. Scrubbing the winter grime off equipment. Carrying plug trays out to the fields. Disposing of the carcasses of young animals that hadn't thrived.

Jessica had learned to live with that too.

The weather had also become an integral part of their lives. The television in the farmhouse stayed tuned to the Weather Channel pretty much every minute of every day. She guessed it was mostly for Nonna, who liked to listen to it from her bedroom. Everyone else used their phones to track the changes in the weather.

"It's my trick knee," moaned Young Billy. "It's tellin' me something."

"What is it saying?"

"When it hurts like this, it means that bad weather's on the way."

Jessica looked at the weather app on her phone. "It says here clear skies, maybe a little rain on Thursday."

"Which app are you using?"

"Weather dot com."

He shook his head. "Monkeys could do a better job forecasting than whoever they got workin' there. Something big's coming."

Jessica turned off the hose. "So that means we'd better do as much tractor work as we can now, right?"

He smiled. "That's right. But the hay isn't ready yet."

"Then can we use the loader for something?"

"I don't know. Ask Stanley."

They turned as the farm manager approached, walking with a barely suppressed swagger. "What's happening here?"

"Is there anything we need to do with the tractor before the rain arrives?" asked Jessica.

He looked confused. "There's no rain coming."

"Yeah there is," said Young Billy. "My knee just started acting up."

"Your knee," said Stanley, shaking his head, "cannot compete with modern meteorology."

"It doesn't lie, boss."

"Maybe you want to go to the doctor? Get that checked out?"

"I've been living with this my whole life. Trust me. It's a dropping barometer. Seventy-two hours until a storm."

"All right," said Stanley, humoring him, "let's pretend there's rain coming. Since you asked, Jessica, there is something you can do."

"What?"

A nasty smile spread across his face. "Scooter's delivering a load of manure in about half an hour. Somebody's got to spread it on sector seven."

Her nose crinkled, but Jessica kept a straight face. "I can do that."

"Are you sure? I can make Ernesto do it. He doesn't mind."

"If you show me how to hook up the spreader to the tractor, I can do it."

Then Jessica's phone sounded. It was Nonna. She'd started using the phone a lot more since becoming bed-ridden.

Jessica picked up. "Yes, Nonna. Right now? Okay. Yes, I'll be right in."

"Nonna?" said Stanley.

"Yep." She stowed the phone away. "She wants to meet with me."

"How fortunate," said Stanley, his voice tinged with mockery. "I'll have Ernesto do it."

"Maybe next time?"

"Sure, Jessica."

Showing willingness to shovel shit was a small victory, but as Jessica walked towards the farmhouse, she thought about how every such victory solidified her place on the family farm.

Chapter Thirty-Seven

NONNA WAS LAYING IN BED, a lace nightgown plunging dangerously low on her chest. An array of papers and file folders were strewn on her lap around the bed. A calculator lay within arm's reach, and a pair of steel-rimmed spectacles was perched on her nose.

"I wanted to talk to you two weeks ago," she said.

Jessica remembered. She's mentioned it on the night that she went to her first class, the night of the goat escape. In the ensuing chaos, she'd forgotten all about the conversation.

"I'm sorry."

Nonna waved off the apology. "Well, this won't come as a shock to you, but this farm isn't doing well."

Jessica dropped into the Queen Anne's chair nearest her grandmother's bed. She pulled off her boots and socks and began massaging her own feet. At times like this, she wished that she had a boyfriend.

"Financially?" said Jessica.

"Yes. Here's why." Nonna picked up a sheaf of papers close to her. "Do you have any idea about the costs that are associated with running a farm?"

"Nope," said Jessica.

"Let me enlighten you." Nonna cleared her throat and began to tick off the bills on her fingers. "Every month, I have to pay the seed companies. Then I have to pay the fertilizer suppliers. Then I have to pay the fuel distributors. I have to pay the insurance agents, the veterinary bills, the property taxes. And the regulators always find something wrong, so there's another fine. Then, after all that is over, I balance my books."

She gestured at her notepad, the small lines of numbers running back and forth on them.

"Is it bad?" said Jessica.

"We didn't break even last year. First time ever. Granted, it wasn't by much, just a few hundred dollars, but still—we *have* to break even. This is a business too."

Jessica sat up, feeling energized. "I suggested to Stanley that we open up the farm to the public. Have Sundays at Nonna's Farms, once a month."

"I'll bet he hated that idea."

"Yeah."

"Stanley doesn't interact well with other people."

"He doesn't have to," said Jessica. "I'll greet the people. You can too."

Nonna took off her glasses. Her eyes looked tired, purple pouches sagging below the bloodshot eyes.

"This farm has never been open to the public," she said.

"Maybe it should be."

"It'll turn into a playscape for children."

"It'll bring in revenue."

"We're not licensed for it."

"I'll get the licenses," said Jessica. "We charge five dollars' admission, do advertising, get some garbage cans, handicapped ramps—"

Nonna sighed, and Jessica stopped the description. "What?"

"I'm old," she said.

"You're only as old as you feel—"

"*And I feel old.*"

Nonna's eyes were burning. Jessica gulped. Her grandmother could be a fearsome woman, when she wanted to be.

"So?"

"I don't have this in me. I can't change things now, at this age."

"Then let me handle it."

Nonna inhaled deeply. "Jessica, there's something else you should know."

"What?"

"I've written Stanley into my will. He's going to receive the farm."

In the chair, Jessica found herself frozen. She couldn't speak, couldn't breathe, couldn't think. Her throat seemed to have swollen to twice its ordinary size.

"I know this is hard to hear," said Nonna.

"Yeah, it is."

"Your mother obviously has never shown any interest. And I thought that we'd lost you to New York City. So, last year, when Stanley asked me about it, it seemed like a good idea to sell to him."

Jessica tried processing this. She couldn't. She simply couldn't fathom Stanley becoming not only the manager, but also the owner, overseer, lord protector, of her family's property.

"He knows this land," said Nonna. "He can be trusted to treat it right."

"Maybe, but—"

"But what? The only other alternative is AgriCon."

"Please don't do *that*," said Jessica.

"Of course not. So this is where we stand."

"What if I wanted to stay here after..." Jessica let the sentence trail off.

"After I'm gone?" finished Nonna.

"Yes."

"Well, that'd be up to him. I don't know what he'd want to do. That's why you have to keep a good relationship with him."

"I could run the farm."

Nonna looked at her with warmth in her eyes. "You're such a sweet thing."

Jessica felt herself growing more emotional. She heard the words begin flying out of her mouth—how much she wanted to live on the farm, to stay on the farm, to preserve it, to manage this legacy that her mother had hated and that she, Jessica, had ignored until now. Pearls of sweat popped onto her upper lip.

When she was finished, Nonna grasped her hand. "Don't ever change," she said.

"I'm serious," replied Jessica.

"So am I, sweetheart. Now, would you fetch me some iced tea. I'm parched."

As Jessica went into the kitchen, she kept turning over in her mind the ways that she might, somehow, someday, prove herself to her own grandmother.

Chapter Thirty-Eight

IN THE SHADE of the storage barn, Jessica was bent over the tractor, her elbows deep inside its guts—and she had zero idea what she was looking at.

Fortunately Young Billy was standing right alongside her. He pointed. "That's the universal joint."

"Okay," she said.

"See that little crank on the side? Turn it three times using—"

"This crank?"

"No, *that*—"

"Oh."

Jessica made three turns with her wrist. "Like that?"

"Yes. Now we're ready to address the PTO shaft."

"What should I call it?"

"Funny. First, switch to a hex-head bolt."

"Okay."

Jessica leapt to her feet and ran over to the toolbox, which was on a table near the open doorway of the storage barn. She began rummaging. "What am I looking for?"

"Six sides," said Young Billy. "That's why it's *hex*."

A movement outside the storage barn caught Jessica's eye. She looked up. A small figure was approaching from the main road. It seemed to be on a bicycle.

"Did you find it?" he said.

"No," she said. "It looks like we have a visitor."

"Who?"

"I don't know."

She stepped outside, feeling the balmy breeze caress her, the gray air plump with humidity.

As the small figure drew closer, she recognized him. It was Mikey.

Wearing a tight bicyclist's shirt and black bicyclist's shorts, he was huffing and puffing as he arrived in the dirt yard. He slowed to a stop, hoisted his leg over the seat, and let the bicycle fall into the dirt.

"You turd," he said, pointing at his bicycle. "You ruined my Saturday."

Jessica unsuccessfully tried to stifle a giggle. He heard her and looked up. "This is how I gently handle all my problems."

"You didn't tell me you were a biker."

"It's a new hobby. Intended to slim and shape."

"I see."

He modeled his new physique for her. "Please, control yourself. We can't all be blessed with such a girlish figure."

Jessica laughed. "Don't you have to work today?"

He looked puzzled. "Today's Saturday."

"Oh." Jessica shook her head. The days of the week had nearly lost all their meaning.

"See, family farmers work so hard they forget what day it is."

"Yeah, there's a lot to do. So what's the reason for your visit?"

Mikey took off his helmet and threw it onto the ground. His hair was sweaty and pointing straight up. "No reason. Just wanted to check out your operation. Maybe pay a visit to Nonna, if she'll have me."

Jessica smiled. "You didn't want to see *me*, of course."

"Nah." He peered around her into the storage barn. "Who's in there? Did I interrupt something?"

Young Billy came into the doorway. "Look at this."

Mikey's face lit up. "Young Billy, long time, no see. What's up?"

He walked over to shake hands, but the older man brought him in for a hug. Then Mikey stepped back while Young Billy looked him up and down.

"You always dress that bad?" said Young Billy.

"Only when it helps me lose weight."

"Good on you. How's things at AgriCon?"

"Awful."

"Why don't you come work for us? We're just fixing the universal joint on the PTO shaft."

Mikey looked at him blankly. "I work in an office."

Jessica said, "Can we take a break, Young Billy?"

"Sure."

Jessica gestured to Mikey. "Let's go for a walk."

They tramped across the meadow, the clover brushing their shoes, towards a small hillock. Jessica led them to a young ash whose branches were just starting to sprout green buds.

Mikey plopped down in the shade, fell back on the grass, and watched the gray clouds billow overhead.

"I make you laugh too much," he said.

"No such thing."

"You probably think I'm a dancing monkey."

"Fine. Entertain me, monkey."

"As long as it doesn't involve fixing a PTO shaft. I studied chemistry for Christ's sake."

They looked out at the green-drenched fields, the sweet, tangy scent of fresh pasture floating on the breeze. A honeybee flew in lazy swirls nearby, searching for new flowers.

"Did you ever think about me?" Mikey said.

"When?"

"I don't know. Some time. When we were teenagers?"

"Sure," she replied. "I mean, we always think about our childhood crushes. What about you?"

In a small voice, he said, "Yeah."

"A lot?"

"Well," he said, picking the head off a dandelion, "when I wasn't busy with all my other girls. And there've been lots, of course."

"Of course," she agreed, smiling.

"But we always think about the one that got away."

"We were six, Mikey."

"Seven. And that's old enough to be tied down."

"For who?" she said, laughing.

"European royalty."

Jessica smiled. "We didn't even know what we were."

He shrugged. "Whatever. We were kids."

"Exactly."

"The bigger question," he said, "is what we are going to become."

Mikey fixed her with a look, and she saw something flash behind his eyes, a long-suppressed passion.

Jessica began to feel unbalanced, even flustered. She suddenly got to her feet. "I don't know," she said, "but I've got to get to work. I'll take you to Nonna before you leave."

"We can hang out a little longer."

"Young Billy's waiting."

"Right," said Mikey, "the galactic joint on the tractor." He stood up, brushing off the bits of hay that had clung to his

Lycra shorts. "Let's find Nonna. She could probably use a bad joke or two."

"And I bet you know some really bad ones."

"Sure do. These clothes, for one."

As they made their way back across the meadow towards the farmhouse, she felt Mikey reach out and grasp her hand—and she was surprised when she let him do it.

Chapter Thirty-Nine

"OKAY," said Jessica, rifling through Young Billy's music collection, "I'd have to say that this one's my favorite."

"Which one?"

She lifted up a compact disc. "This one. You played it last week while we were greasing the hay equipment."

They were in the living room of the farmhouse, relaxing after a long day's work. It'd been a physical day. Together she and Young Billy had repaired the tractor, cleared brush, augured nearly fifty new post holes along the edge of the property to replace an aging perimeter fence, begun to re-mineralize a fallow field, and cleaned the newly-empty greenhouse. Jessica's body ached from head to toe, but it was a good ache, well-earned.

He peered at the cover. "That's Blake Shelton's greatest hits."

"It's really good."

Young Billy smirked slightly. "You said you didn't really like his music."

"When did I say that?"

"When I picked you up from the airport a month ago. Remember?"

Jessica struggled to recall. One month felt like a lifetime; the person she'd been back at *Spretza*, a distant memory.

Four weeks ago, she'd been wet behind the ears, unable to stand on her own two feet. Now, after four weeks of learning, of work, of baptism by fire, Jessica felt that she was finally pitching in.

At the music cabinet, she slipped the disc into the player and punched play. Soon the twangy sounds of a classic country song issued from the speakers. *Come on, somebody, why don't you run, Ole Red's itchin' to have a little fun.*

"I love the lyrics," Jessica said, raising her voice over the music.

"Shelton didn't write 'em," said Young Billy.

"No?"

"Kenny Rogers did. It's a cover song."

Jessica began a classic country slide in her sock-feet on the bare wood flooring. "Well, I don't care, this is a good song."

"Hey, you move pretty good, girl," said Young Billy.

"Let's see your moves."

He hoisted himself up out of the couch and began to match her country slide. Soon she saw that he was far better than she was.

"You're full of surprises," she said.

"Years of practice. It's the only thing I can do."

He spun Jessica around, and she shrieked in delight. They whirled over the floorboards. They kicked aside the throw rug. They boot-scoot-and-boogied across the house.

"Let's go country line-dancing!" she said.

"Only in Nashville," he replied. "That's the only place I'll do it."

"Then let's go there. Right now."

"That's three states and four tanks of gas away."

Jessica was swaying her hips left and right, when a shadow fell across the floor. She glanced up.

Nonna was standing in the doorway, in her old dressing gown. A grim set to her lips told Jessica that something was wrong.

"What's the matter?" she said. "Is the music too loud?"

Her grandmother shuffled across the floor, cane in hand, looking older than ever. Young Billy stepped aside as she passed.

She went to the cabinet and shut off the music. The thick, humming silence of nighttime on the farm crawled in from the windows.

"I enjoy Mister Shelton's music," said Nonna, "but I have news that's more important."

"What is it?"

"Your mother is coming. I just found out."

Jessica felt her throat go as dry as sandpaper. "When?"

"Right now."

"They're driving here *right now*?"

Nonna nodded. "As we speak. Chase got three days off yesterday, his boss said use it or lose it. So they're on their way."

Jessica leaned against the chair for support. Memories of her mother flashed through her mind's eye—ugly images, angry words, promises unfulfilled, lessons learned.

"She can't come without him?" Jessica said.

Nonna shook her head sadly. "You know your mother."

"Why would she *want* to come here?" snapped Jessica. "What could she *want* from us? She's *never* liked this farm. She ran away from here as soon as she could."

Her grandmother fixed her with a faraway look. "I think she wants to see you, dear."

Feeling her mood crater, Jessica rubbed the bridge of her nose with her fingers. "I'm really not ready for this."

"Well, you have about an hour to somehow get yourself ready. Young Billy, can you help me make up the spare room?"

He nodded. "Yes, ma'am."

They retreated into the back of the house, and Jessica slumped at the kitchen table, left alone with her thoughts.

Chapter Forty

YELLOW DISHWASHING GLOVES on her hands, Jessica was finishing the last of the cups when she heard her mother's car pull up into the dirt yard.

Her nose twitched. Reaching into the cupboard, she grabbed six clean plates, six clean cups, and a handful of clean silverware. She dumped them all into the soapy tub of water. That would keep her busy for the next fifteen minutes.

She heard the sounds of the arrival. The footsteps on the front porch. The screen door screeching open. Nonna saying, *Hello, welcome, it's been so long*. A man grunting in response. That would be Chase.

Then an awkward silence.

"Where is Jessica?" said a woman's voice.

Jessica stopped. It was the first time that she had heard her mother's voice in two years. A plate slipped from her fingers and smashed on the floor.

"She's finishing up the dishes," said Nonna.

"Sounds like she's finished breaking them," said the man. "Where I come from, it's rude for a girl to ignore her mother."

In the kitchen, crouched on the floor and picking up the

pieces of the broken crockery, Jessica gritted her teeth. Chase was already making her blood boil, and they hadn't even spoken yet.

"I can go and get her," said Nonna.

Jessica heard her grandmother shuffle into the kitchen. "Jessica, your mother's here. Come out and say hello."

"In a minute," she said.

"Come say hello. Don't be rude."

She couldn't disobey Nonna. It was easier to force the sun below the horizon at noon. Jessica tossed the cup that she had been washing into the sink and followed her grandmother out into the main room, holding her sudsy yellow gloves away from her body.

Her mother was standing there. She looked smaller than ever, a ghost fluttering in the shadow of her large boyfriend. Chase himself hadn't changed a bit—bald-headed, beady little eyes, a body full of tense, knotted muscles.

"Hi," said Jessica flatly.

"Nice to see you, Jessica," he said. It sounded forced. "Back from the city, I see."

"Yep."

Her mother didn't say a word. She couldn't even meet Jessica's eyes.

"Go on, Barbara," ordered Chase, "hug your daughter."

Her mother tentatively stepped forward. Jessica reluctantly opened her arms, like a cactus, holding the sudsy yellow gloves up to the ceiling.

Then Jessica felt the slight woman wrap her arms tightly around her own torso. Her feeling of desperation was as palpable as her ribcage. There was almost nothing left of the woman, not after the years of substance abuse and physical abuse and spiritual neglect.

"Hi mom," she said.

"Jessica," came the muffled reply.

She stood there awkwardly for another few seconds, until Chase pulled her mother away with a rough hand. "That's enough, Barbara."

Now the four of them stood together uneasily. Jessica was aware of the labored breathing, the four sets of lungs.

"So where should I take our bags?" said Chase.

"Into the spare bedroom," said Nonna. "Jessica's staying in the attic."

"You always liked it there, didn't you?" said her mother.

"Yep," replied Jessica. She felt like someone had poured a solid block of concrete in her into her heart.

"You planning on staying long, Jessica?" said Chase.

"I'm not sure," she said. "I just want to keep the farm on its feet while Nonna recovers."

"That's nice of you," he replied evenly.

Her mother said nothing, her vacant eyes stared at the far wall.

"I'm going to finish the dishes," she said.

Jessica swiveled on her heel, flew back into the kitchen, and leaned against the refrigerator. This wasn't going to be easy.

Chapter Forty-One

JESSICA FINISHED THE DISHES AND, blaming exhaustion, headed straight upstairs into the attic. She shut the door and lay down on her mattress. The hole in the ceiling gaped above her, the stuffed rags reminding her that temporary fixes never lasted, that big problems couldn't be avoided forever.

She balled up her fists and closed her eyes.

Downstairs, she could hear their hushed conversation. Nonna's murmuring, Chase's grunts, her mother's silence.

She didn't want any of this.

Then, from outside the house, she heard a whistle. The type of whistle that Ernesto made to cattle when he wanted their attention.

Jessica bolted off the bed, went over to the window, and looked out. The farmhand was below her window, hiding in the darkness. She could see him trying to avoid the light from the kitchen below.

She lifted the window. "I'm not a cow, Ernesto."

"But it got your attention," he whispered.

"What do you want?"

"Come with me. I want to show you something."

"Now?"

"Of course."

"I can't."

"Why?"

"My mother is downstairs."

"And?"

"She'll want to talk."

"You don't want to talk with your mother?"

Jessica shook her head. "It's complicated."

Ernesto thought for a moment. "Then just come out through the window."

"From here?"

"Yes. Wait, I'll get the ladder."

Jessica watched Ernesto head off to the storage shed. He reappeared a moment later empty-handed.

"Where is it?" she whispered.

"It's gone. Stanley probably left it near the willows after trimming today."

"Never mind then," she said.

Ernesto looked desperate. "Please. You can jump off the roof."

"Are you out of your mind?"

"No, my mind is okay. I will catch you."

Jessica sighed. She was starting to feel like a teenage girl being wooed by her secret suitor. It wasn't necessarily a bad feeling.

"Hold on," she said. She ran to her dresser and donned a long-sleeved shirt, then a jacket, then her sneakers.

She returned to the window, crawled outside onto the roof, clambered over to the eave, and peered down at him.

Ernesto widened his stance, tugged up the thighs of his jeans, the sleeves of his coat. He held his arms out. "You can trust me," he said. "Remember how I trusted you?"

Jessica thought about that. Then she drew a breath, rolled to the edge of the roof, swung her body over the edge, dangled from the rain gutter by her fingertips for a moment, and let go.

She felt his strong arms grab her around the waist, then quickly lower her to the ground. A moment later, she was on her feet, shocked at how easy it was.

"That felt like ballet," she said.

He grinned. "Maybe we should take a dance class."

"Maybe."

He held a finger up to his lips. "Keep your voice down and follow me."

Beneath the full moon, they crept away from the house and across the property, past the chicken coops, down the steep incline, past the soggy ditch that she'd driven the tractor into headfirst, past the apple orchard. It was a fifteen-minute walk, and soon they were at the farthest portion of Nonna's property.

"This had better be good," she said.

"It is," said Ernesto.

They arrived at a small hillock nestled within a copse of trees. It was unassuming, about twenty feet high, no bigger around than a couple of cars, and covered in wild grasses. On Nonna's property, Jessica had noticed at least a dozen other similar ones. Jessica hadn't ever paid too much attention to them.

"This is it," said Ernesto.

"This hill?"

"Does it look suspicious to you?"

"How can a hill be suspicious?"

"It's symmetrical."

She tilted her head. The brambles, wild grasses, and branches nearly obscured its true shape. "I can't tell."

Then Ernesto pointed to the left, towards another small

hillock about fifty meters away. "You see that one? It's symmetrical too."

Jessica stood there, squinting at the dark mound across the pale-white moonlit orchard. "Huh."

Then Ernesto turned and pointed to the right. "And there's another one along the perimeter fence—"

Jessica suddenly snapped her fingers. "The one by the road. I know that one. I used to play on it."

Ernesto nodded. "Did you ever notice that they're all the same size?"

"Weird."

"And they're all in a line." He used his arm to illustrate the same axis.

Jessica looked at all of them. Ernesto was totally right.

"Holy crap," she said.

The farmhand was looking at her. "Do you know what this means?"

"I think so."

"Tell me."

She poked him in the chest with a finger. "No, you tell *me*."

Ernesto giggled. It was the first time she'd ever heard him make a sound like that. "It means don't be so loud—or you'll *wake up the dead*."

He dangled his fingers in front of her eyes. Jessica slugged him in the chest. "Stop saying that! Maybe it's something else."

Ernesto shook his head. "Nature doesn't make straight lines."

Jessica chewed on her lip, crossed one boot behind the other. She felt a sudden attraction towards this man.

"You could've brought me here during the day," she said.

"We're too busy working."

"Plus it's scarier this way."

"Yes."

"And if I got scared enough," she continued, "you thought that I'd jump into your arms."

A guilty smile spread across Ernesto's face. "You are presuming too much from me."

A loud snap sounded from the orchard behind them. Startled, Jessica leapt into Ernesto's arms. He caught her, for the second time that night. She caught the scent of rich earth and crackling campfire.

"It's a deer," he said. "Look."

She turned and looked into the silent moonlit orchard. The thin four-legged creature was pulling at a branch.

"If he waits until fall, he'll have a much better snack."

"He's young and doesn't know any better," said Ernesto.

His arm stayed wrapped around her waist. Jessica felt her heartbeat throbbing in her chest.

"Ernesto—"

"Shh," he said.

He swiveled her around, and she found herself, eyes closed, in a crushingly sweet first kiss, under the moonlight.

When he tried to pull away, she gripped his arms and brought him back, leaning her face into his chest. His nose felt cold, but his lips were warm.

"That was nice," she said.

"It was very good," he replied.

She felt a sudden panic. "We should go back. I'm getting cold. But I really don't want to talk my mother."

"It doesn't matter."

"Why?"

He smiled. "You can't get back up to the roof without the ladder."

Chapter Forty-Two

BACK AT THE FARMHOUSE, Nonna's light was off. It was already way past her grandmother's bedtime.

Jessica took off her boots on the porch, gently swung open the front door, and tiptoed into the farmhouse, taking care to keep the door from screeching behind her.

Then, while crossing the kitchen, she suddenly sensed that she wasn't alone.

In a corner of the darkness, her mother said, "I hope you didn't stay up too late."

Jessica's heart nearly leaped out of her chest. She reached for the lintel of the doorframe. "*Jesus*, you scared me."

"Don't say that word too loud. Chase doesn't like it."

"Should I say Allah instead?"

"He doesn't like that either. He's real religious." Her mother paused. "It's okay with me, though."

A small blue light appeared in the darkness, dimly illuminating her mother's face. Jessica recognized it as an e-cigarette.

"You like those?"

"This is the only fun Chase lets me have."

Jessica turned on a small lamp, yellow light forming a cone around them, protecting against the darkness. She tried to keep her voice even. "You've had a lot of fun in your life, Barbara."

Her mother didn't wince. Jessica had begun calling her *Barbara* years earlier, to needle her, to imply that she wasn't any sort of authority figure.

"Can you keep me company for a minute?" replied her mother. "I haven't been sleeping very well."

Jessica sat down restively at the kitchen table, one sock-foot bouncing on the floor. She kept her coat on. "What would you like to talk about?"

"Tell me about New York."

Jessica shrugged. "I went there. I worked. I left."

"The magazine job—"

"*Spretza* was sold to another company. My boss told me to leave."

Her mother's eyes were blue and flat. They didn't search or probe. They had always been like that, a little watery and unfocused.

"You're at that time in your life," she said. "All the important decisions are being made."

Jessica nodded. For a moment, the only sound was the ticking of the clock on the wall of the kitchen.

Her mother cleared her throat. "Shit, say something else."

"What do you want me to say? That I'm becoming my own person?"

Her mother's glassy eyes focused on Jessica for a moment. Then she looked off into the darkness. "I've never learned how to do that. I guess some of us just need other people a little more." She took another drag off the e-cigarette. "It's so hard for us to be alone."

"It's hard for *you*," said Jessica.

Her mother shrugged. "I've always been looking for someone to save me. I can admit it. I know it's weak, but that's just how I've always felt."

"Well, don't look at me," said Jessica.

"You don't have to save me," replied her mother, "at least not while I've got Chase."

"Maybe."

"He's given me everything." Barbara's hands were shaking slightly. "He's given more than a woman like me could've ever hoped for."

These weren't new revelations. Jessica had known for a long time that her mother valued her boyfriend more highly than she valued Jessica. In fact, it was a relief to hear it stated so openly.

Then she yawned. "I'm sorry, it's been a long day."

"So you're fitting in well here? Life on the farm?"

"Of course," said Jessica. "I already lived here for two years when I was a kid."

The glazed look in her mother's eyes told Jessica that she'd forgotten about that, which meant that she'd also forgotten why it'd happened. Jessica shook her head sadly. The drugs, the mental breakdown, the physical abuse—all of it had broken Barbara. She'd been unable to care for her only daughter, and now, as an older woman, she couldn't even remember much from that period.

"So you did," said her mother, as though from a distance. "This farm is where you found your heaven."

Jessica stood up. "I have to wake up in five hours."

"I suppose," said her mother. "We only see each other once every couple of years. Oh, Nonna says be sure to close your window. She says that rain is coming."

Jessica, already on her way towards the stairway, paused. "She said that?"

"Young Billy told her so, and she believes him over the official forecast."

"Huh."

Nonna was nothing if not pragmatic. As she went upstairs, Jessica began to think about what tomorrow would hold.

Chapter Forty-Three

THE MORNING BROKE chill and gray, no more than fifty-five degrees, and under the dark skies, Jessica moved the four chicken coops. This time, however, she filled the feeders with twice as much feed as usual. When she had finished, she looked at the eastern horizon. It was a solid wall of black clouds.

As she returned to the main farmhouse, she saw Stanley in the dirt yard, tinkering with what seemed to be a yellow engine caged inside an aluminum frame. It was mounted on a pair of wheels.

"This might sound obvious," she said, "but there's a bad storm coming."

"I know," replied Stanley. "The forecast changed. Young Billy was right."

"Do you know how bad it's going to be?"

His voice was tight and clipped. "Let's just say I'm glad that we're not living next to the river."

Then Jessica recognized the device. It was a generator. She chewed her lip. "So what can we do? Nail plywood to the windows?"

"No, it's supposed to be more rain than wind. Right now, Young Billy is shutting off the gas. I don't know what you can do. Maybe you could find the hand fuel pump."

"What does it look like?"

"It's orange. It has a hand crank."

"Does it really exist?"

He glanced up at her. "Yes, Jessica. No more games."

"Okay."

"After that, you can secure anything you see lying around. Then you can clear out the debris from the drainage ditches along the road. We don't need anything clogging up the municipal sewage lines and backing up onto our property."

Jessica nodded. "Thank you for trusting me."

"Sure."

She kept looking at him. He noticed her staring. "What?"

"Nothing."

He took off his glasses and spoke very carefully. "Jessica, your contributions are valued. We appreciate you."

That was startling. Stanley had seemed, for the first time, to understand what she wanted to hear, needed to hear.

"Thank you again," she said.

He returned to fine-tuning the generator, and Jessica began tidying up the dirt yard. She was feeling, finally, like part of the team. She picked up crates and stacked them in the storage shed. She lifted anything that looked even vaguely electronic off the ground.

As she used a rake to clean out the ditches near the road, the first raindrop spattered on her cheek.

She looked up. The silver thunderhead was snarling the sky above her head, coiling and twisting like an epic snake in ancient mythology. Another drop hit her in the forehead.

Jessica had begun walking back to the farmhouse when the heavens began to open up. She broke into a run.

She vaulted onto the front porch just as the sheets really hit. Turning around, breathing heavily, she watched her first rural rainstorm in nearly twenty years.

And it was a big one.

Chapter Forty-Four

FOR THE NEXT SIX HOURS, massive sheets of rain pounded the rooftop, drumming the walls, churning up the dirt.

Inside the farmhouse, Jessica had retreated into Nonna's bedroom. She had lit a pair of candlesticks, dimmed the lights, and curled up in the Queen Anne's chair with a cup of tea, watching the water splash the windows.

"Dear," said Nonna, knitting in bed, "tell me what you're thinking about?"

"Not much."

"Rainy days are good for spilling one's heart."

"The future."

Nonna's fingers clack-clacked on her knitting needles. "At my age, I don't think about the future. There's so much more behind me to think about."

"Oh."

"But since we're discussing the future, would you be willing to stay here on the farm?"

"I think so," said Jessica.

"It's not a small decision."

"I haven't decided yet."

"Well," said Nonna, reaching for her tea, "don't rush it. The question will answer itself. At least, that's what I've always thought."

"What do you mean?"

"The big questions in life answer themselves. The small questions are the ones we agonize over."

"I disagree. I agonize over all of them."

Nonna laughed. "If you climb to the mountaintop, don't reject the sage's advice."

Jessica smiled and wiggled her toes. She felt extraordinarily safe right now—cared for, protected, loved. She couldn't imagine leaving this place, wanted it to always stay the same.

She stared out the window. A deep, wide puddle of muddy water had formed in front of the entrance to the goat enclosure. "It's really coming down out there," said Jessica.

"That's a waste of words," muttered her grandmother.

"Words are cheap."

"No," said Nonna, "words *aren't* cheap. That's what city people don't understand. Imagine if I started calling you Kristen."

"I wouldn't like it."

"Exactly. Your name has value. It's just one word."

Jessica decided to change the subject. "What's the worst rainstorm you can remember?"

"Nineteen eighty-two. It ruined half my crops."

"But you survived."

"Barely. These springtime storms have always been bad, but now they're getting more frequent. In other seasons too."

"Young Billy says that too," said Jessica.

"It's worrisome."

"I cleaned up all the debris and lifted the electronics off the ground."

"Thank you, dear, but that's not what I'm worried about."

"What are you worried about?"

Nonna frowned. "I'm worried that since the ground is still hard, it won't absorb this rain. It's going to bounce right off the earth like concrete."

Jessica thought about this. "So where will the water go?"

"Into the creeks."

The implications of that hung in the air. They heard the front door swing open from the other end of the house. Heavy boots clomped down the hallway.

Into the doorway of the bedroom came Young Billy, wearing a yellow raincoat. He was soaked, his short black hair plastered down wetly against his head. He leaned against the doorjamb. "It's been three inches already, Nonna. Forecast says four more inches by this evening. Eight more by tomorrow morning."

Nonna set down her knitting. "Good Lord," she said.

"I'm thinking about the Kilkenny's."

"They're not going to leave," said Nonna.

"They'll have to."

"What's happening?" said Jessica.

"The Kilkenny farm flooded last year," said Nonna.

"I heard," said Jessica. She remembered meeting them while looking for that ridiculous imaginary packet of tomato seeds. She remembered Mary's meekness, her husband Richard confined to a wheelchair.

"That was only seven inches," said Young Billy, "and in the autumn too."

Jessica thought about that. This was twice as much rain, on ground that was apparently much less absorbent. "So what do you suggest?" she said.

"I say we go over there and talk to them. Suggest they move to safer ground for a little while," he said.

"It'll be dangerous getting there," said Nonna.

"Not yet. Later tonight, yes."

Jessica remembered the drive to their house, the newly built bridge over the creek. "Can't you call them?"

"They're not picking up," replied Young Billy. He sighed. "I've spoken to them many times about this. They know where the community stands."

"You should just go," said Nonna. A glint of steel appeared in her eye. "This isn't the time for politeness. If they're too stubborn to ask for help, you need to be a bit more forceful with the offer."

"I understand," said Young Billy.

"Tell them they can stay here if they need."

"Where?" said Jessica.

"I don't know," snapped Nonna, "but we'll make room."

"Are you coming?" said Young Billy. He was looking at Jessica.

Jessica pointed to her own sternum. "Me? Why?"

"Maybe you can talk some sense to Mary. Stanley is coming too."

Jessica shrugged. "All right."

Nonna cut in. "You'll need another big man to lift Richard out of his chair. Stanley and Jessica are both too small."

They all fell silent. "What about Chase?" said Jessica.

"You can ask him," said Nonna. "He and Barbara are in their bedroom. They haven't come out all morning."

"I'll go and ask," said Jessica.

She slid off the chair, padded down the hallway in her slippers, and rapped on her mother's door.

She heard footsteps on the floorboards. Then a man's voice said, "Who is it?"

Jessica rolled her eyes. "It's me. I have a question."

The door opened. Chase was standing there in chinos and a neatly pressed plaid shirt. "What is it," he said.

Jessica peered past him. Her mother was sprawled on the bed, looking disconsolate, a ragdoll that had been flung aside by an indifferent god.

"So we're going to the Kilkenny property," she said, "and we might need a pair of strong arms."

He grew instantly suspicious. "What for?"

"We may have to lift a handicapped man out of his chair, into the truck. He's heavy."

"Is he in trouble?"

"The creek's going to flood. If we don't yank him out now, he might be stranded."

Chase seemed to grow taller, his chest grow larger. "That sounds like something that I can help with."

"Great," said Jessica, "but we have to go right now."

"No," said her mother's voice from the bed.

"I'm sorry, Barbara?" said Jessica.

Her mother lifted the blanket off her head. Her face was wracked with pain. "I don't want Chase to leave me."

Jessica bristled. This was the mother she'd remembered, the mother that she'd been avoiding.

"It's only for an hour."

Barbara shook her head. "I don't want to be alone. What don't you understand about that? Why can't any of you understand that?"

"Now, Barbara," said Chase, "these people need me."

"And you won't be alone," said Jessica. "Nonna's in her room right down the hall."

Her mother crossed her arms. She looked like a small child. "I need him here. Don't you dare take him away from me."

There was no reasoning with her. Jessica remembered this type of demanding behavior well, where are you going, you need to stay here, I hate you, don't leave me like this.

Nothing had changed.

Chase glanced apologetically at Jessica. "I should probably stay."

"She's all yours."

Jessica reached for the doorknob, managed a brief smile, and said goodbye.

Chapter Forty-Five

THE WINDSHIELD of Young Billy's truck was awash in rainwater. Though he'd put the setting on high, the wipers merely threw the water back and forth across the glass. It was like trying to see through a frosted shower door.

"Should we turn around?" said Jessica from the backseat.

"Nuh-uh," said Young Billy, "I could drive these roads blind."

"You basically are," added Stanley.

Jessica drummed her fingers on her knee. "So when we get there, what exactly are we going to do?"

"Think of it like moving an elderly person into an old-folks home," said Stanley. "You convince them that it's for their own good."

"And if it doesn't work?" she said. "We don't have power-of-attorney."

"Then we just pick them up," said Young Billy.

"Literally," said Stanley.

The truck turned past the sign marked Kilkenny's Seeds, which was barely visible through the rainy gray wash on the windows and jounced down the muddy road. The rain had pocked holes in the mud that were big enough to break an axle in.

Then they came to the creek.

What had once been a mere trickle was now a raging whitewater. Its brown, churning surface powered mere inches below the rebuilt concrete bridge.

"Holy cow," said Stanley, "it's almost covered."

"Better get across now."

Young Billy gunned the accelerator, and the truck sped across the bridge in the blink of an eye. Jessica tightened her grip on the arm rest as she felt the tires slip on the slick cement below.

Then they were over it, the creek rushing along to her left, its waters dipping, rising, crashing, already spilling out over its banks and lapping at the edge of the dirt road. She saw just how vulnerable the Kilkennys were to nature and understood how their fields had been wiped out.

The truck cruised up to the side of the farmhouse. The rocking chair on the porch was empty, but Jessica could see the faint outline of a figure inside the screen door.

"Ready to make a run?" said Stanley.

"Yep," said Young Billy.

All three of them popped out of the truck, slammed the doors, and sprinted onto the porch. Jessica was soaked in an instant.

"Holy moly," said Stanley, shaking the water off his head. "That's the worst I've ever seen it."

Young Billy knocked on the screen door. "Mary? Richard?"

The figure appeared again. It was Mary, wearing the same calico jumper, the same raggedy ponytail—but this time there was a grim set to her lips.

"I suppose you're here to yank us off our land," she said.

"Call it what you may," said Young Billy, "we're just worried we might lose you."

"Well, you can just keep driving," she said.

Mary still hadn't opened the door yet. Stanley looked past her into the house. "Richard, you in there?"

A voice sounded from the distant rear of the house. "Stanley?"

"Come out here, you old dog," he said.

As the sheets of rain hammered on the rooftop, Jessica saw the silhouette of the large man in his wheelchair slowly roll into sight.

"Goll darn," said Richard, "the whole welcoming committee is here. You all must be really worried." He tipped his head towards Young Billy and Jessica. "Sir, miss."

"You're aware that it's raining," said Stanley.

"We are," said Richard.

"You're aware that eight more inches are projected by morning?"

"That much?" he said. He looked at his wife. "You didn't say that."

Mary stammered a response. "I might've misheard the report. I thought it was only three."

Young Billy interrupted. "Your bridge is nearly covered."

That did it. Richard wheeled himself around. "Well, shit, let's get out of here. I ain't drowning in this rathole. Make sure you get the emergency pack, Mary."

A low, depressed look hung off Mary's face. "This is *my farm*. My family's property. Five generations."

"It always will be," said Young Billy.

"It's just going to be a very wet farm for a while," added Stanley.

Jessica joined the chorus. "Please come with us, Mary. Nonna says you can stay at our place."

Mary chewed on her lip. Her eyes were glistening with tears. Jessica could see how strong her bond with the land was.

"Well, I'll need to find our emergency pack. And our medication. And our pictures."

Young Billy peered into their living room. "Can we lift your television off the floor?"

"I would like that very much," she said.

Mary opened the door and stepped aside for the visitors.

Chapter Forty-Six

HALF AN HOUR LATER, Jessica was back in the truck, bouncing down the muddy road, the creek to her right. It had swollen even higher in the last thirty minutes, roiling with sluices and peaks and even tiny whitecaps. It was spilling regularly now onto the road.

Behind them was the Kilkennys' truck. It was a white Ford, nearly twenty years old now, fingers of rust reaching up from beneath the underbelly. That was from the salt that was spread out on the roads in the winter.

Stanley craned his head, peering through the windshield. Then he pounded his fist on the dashboard. "Aw crap," he said. "Just what I was afraid of."

Jessica followed his gaze. They were facing the roaring creek now—and the bridge was nowhere to be seen.

"It's gone," said Young Billy.

"No," said Stanley, "it's not gone. Look."

Inside the cab, they all leaned forward. A chuck of water was spraying into the air, long and straight.

"The bridge is still there," said Stanley. "It's about a foot underwater."

"Are you sure?" said Jessica.

"It's new construction. It won't wash away that easily. Go test it if you want to be sure."

"How?"

Stanley frowned. "I don't know. Use a stick."

Jessica figured somebody had to. Drawing a deep breath, she hoisted her jacket over her head and hopped out of the cab into the pouring rain. She picked up a long branch and ran to the creek. Only ten seconds, and she was already drenched.

She stood at the edge of the water, feeling its primeval force rushing past the tip of her boot. This was a flash flood and was highly unpredictable. It could be up to her knees in a second.

Jessica leaned forward and poked the stick down into the brown churn. She felt it hit something hard. She dragged the stick left and right. The tip of the branch was dragging on what seemed to be cement.

As usual, Stanley had been right. The bridge was still there.

A voice behind her said, "It's sturdy. My brother-in-law built it."

Jessica turned. Mary had joined her. The Kilkenny's truck was idling next to their own.

"Should we risk crossing it?"

Mary looked concerned. "Richard thinks we'll be marooned if we don't."

"Thank God for four-wheel drive."

"Speak for yourself," replied Mary, "ours is rear wheel."

"Can you make it?"

"I don't know."

"You can get inside our truck, if you want."

"No," said Mary, steeling herself, "our Ford has gotten through worse spots than this. But then again, it was always Richard driving. I'm not as good as he used to be."

"Let's not stand around getting wet," said Jessica. "We'll go first."

"All right," said Mary.

They returned to their vehicles. Jessica climbed into the cab and wiped the water off her face.

"So?" said Stanley.

"You were right. It's about a foot underwater."

Young Billy nodded. "This truck weighs more than two thousand pounds, plus our weight. It'll get across fine."

Stanley was looking at the white Ford. "Not so sure about that one."

"Mary seems confident," said Jessica.

"They could take the truck back to the house and then cross with us," said Stanley.

"I offered. She said no."

Stanley shrugged. "All right. Hit it."

Jessica held her breath and leaned forward as Young Billy put the truck into first gear and gently eased it into the water. The brown water sluiced hard against the left side of the truck. Jessica could feel its force, but the truck remained solid.

"Keep it centered," said Stanley.

"I know, boss."

As soon as the rear wheels had entered the water—the most dangerous moment—

Young Billy gunned the engine. The truck leapt forward, sending half-moons of water arcing out from each wheel like four wings of water.

A moment later, they were across the flooded bridge, on the solid mud, and Young Billy circled the truck around so they could watch the Kilkennys.

Stanley clapped Young Billy on the shoulder. "Good on you. Where'd you learn to drive like that?"

"Practice."

Jessica exhaled and settled back. "You're the best."

Young Billy tipped his cap at her in the rearview mirror. "Ready for round two."

They watched the old white Ford approach the edge of the flooding creek. Behind the wheel, Mary's face was a tight mask of fear. In the passenger seat, Richard was gesturing violently.

"Come on, Mary," whispered Young Billy.

"Find the gas pedal," said Stanley.

At last, the truck nosed its front wheels into the river. The brown water rushed up its wheels and into the engine block. Then it stopped.

"Keep moving," said Young Billy.

"She can't find traction," said Stanley.

Jessica peered at the rear of the truck. Its back wheels were spinning in the mud, trying to gain some purchase.

And that's when she noticed the hood of the Ford beginning to drift to the left.

Downriver.

Through the windshield, Mary's face was frozen in fear. Richard was screaming now, pounding on the dashboard. The rear wheels spun faster—

—they finally caught—

—and the truck moved out into the river.

At a slight angle.

"Shit," said Stanley.

The front right wheel of the truck suddenly dove below the water. The rear left part of the truck lifted up into the air, brown water arcing up and into the bed of the vehicle. Inside the cab, Richard's hands reached out and pressed against the windshield, his mouth screaming. Mary had gone ghastly white, her skinny arms frantically trying to turn the wheel.

"Did she just drive off the bridge?" asked Jessica.

"Yeah," Young Billy. "The truck probably doesn't weigh enough."

"What are we going to do?"

Young Billy opened his door. "Help them."

Chapter Forty-Seven

JESSICA AND STANLEY followed him out of the cab and down to the edge of the swollen creek. The white truck was less than fifteen feet away, but between them was a brown rush of water powerful enough to knock Jessica off her feet.

Young Billy had pulled a rope from his truck and was tying it around his waist. He threw the other end to Stanley, who wound it around his arm.

"Are you sure?" said Stanley.

"I weigh two hundred and forty pounds," said Young Billy. "This little dribble won't do a thing to me. Heads up, Mary's coming out first."

He plunged a foot into the water. The torrent sluiced around his leg. Jessica noticed that it went up to nearly his knee. The creek had risen even in the last two minutes.

Young Billy plunged his other foot into the water and stood there, getting a sense of things, his arms spread out for balance. Then he began to walk, one foot lifted totally out of the water and placed down. It was a slow progress, but in this way he made it to the side of the truck and opened the passenger door.

Mary's face was pure shock as he reached in, gripped her behind the back and under the knees, and pulled her bodily out of the driver's seat.

Jessica watched in admiration as this big man, this gentle giant, slowly high-stepped his way back to the bank. He set Mary down in the mud. Jessica put an arm around her.

"Oh my goodness," said Mary. "You *have* to get Richard."

"Comin' right up," said Young Billy.

He turned and crossed back into the river, high stepping back to the truck. He reached into the open door. Jessica could hear him shouting something at Richard, who was still in the passenger seat.

Young Billy evidently didn't like the response, because he leaned into the truck and across the seat, clamped his large hands onto Richard, and hauled the stricken man across the bench seat and out of the truck. Crouching, he then slid Richard's incapacitated body onto his own shoulders.

Jessica felt her fists clench. Richard Kilkenny, even now, still weighed as much as Young Billy himself. It wouldn't be easy carrying anything that heavy through raging knee-high waters.

Young Billy turned and took his first high step. His left leg came down unsteadily, swaying a little bit as he struggled beneath the load.

He took a second step. Jessica watched his body quaver with the effort.

On the third step, the force of the torrent was too strong. His left knee gave out, his left foot sliding beneath the right leg —and in the blink of an eye he'd fallen onto his side. Poor Richard yelped as the man beneath him toppled, and a second later he'd pitched sideways into the current too.

"Oh!" shouted Mary.

Stanley was already two steps into the water, but his slight build was wobbling in the brown rush. He reached out a hand to Richard, who grabbed it, and pulled the handicapped man across the brown roiling water to the bank of the creek, where Jessica and Mary took one arm each and dragged him to safety. There, he lay gasping in the mud and the rain, like the victim of a war.

"Oh baby," said Mary, cradling her husband's head, "thank heavens you're okay."

"This isn't worth it," he said. "I want off this land."

"We're leaving in a minute."

"No," said Richard, "I want to sell this property."

His eyes were rounded and intense. This sounded like a big discussion, and a private one too, so Jessica backed away from the couple. She looked back to the creek.

Their truck had turned forty-five degrees now, and the cab was utterly filled with dirty, foaming water. She watched a paper coffee cup floating against the windshield. Jessica felt their devastation. Their truck was ruined.

Meanwhile, Young Billy was heavy enough to have sat down in the creek, his back to the torrent, a giant scallop of brown water fanning across his broad shoulders. He was clutching his knee. Stanley was lurching around in the current, off-balance, trying to reach him.

"Is he injured?" shouted Jessica.

Stanley shrugged. He finally reached Young Billy, bent over at the waist, and exchanged a few words that Jessica couldn't hear. Then he crouched next to Young Billy, put his shoulder underneath the wounded man's armpit, and tried to hoist him to his feet.

It wasn't easy. Young Billy had six inches and at least eighty pounds on his boss. They failed once, tried again, failed a second time, and then made a third attempt.

This time, they managed to stay upright. Leaning on each other, the two began to high step through the current. Jessica watched anxiously as Young Billy leaned on the farm manager, wincing with each step.

Then she glimpsed something upstream.

A log.

A heavy branch, forked and spiked, it was at least ten feet long and was being carried madly down the swollen creek, wiping out the crested whitecaps, sailing mightily over the dips. It was unstoppable.

And it was heading for Stanley and Young Billy.

"Watch out!" Jessica shouted, pointing.

Stanley heard her warning. Following her finger, he swung his head and saw the impending hazard, but it was too late. In the blink of an eye, the massive branch had swept sideways into both of them.

Young Billy howled as it collided into his damaged left knee. He threw his arms into the air, lost his balance, and fell backwards—

—smashing the back of his head onto the open truck door.

Stanley, being smaller, was utterly wiped out by the heavy branch. It knocked him onto his belly, then rolled over his back, pushing him underwater, and carried him twenty feet downstream. When at last his face emerged from the water, it was wearing a look of sheer panic.

All of this was happening right in front of Jessica, but there was nothing she could do. She'd be swept away the moment she tried to interfere.

Then she looked back at Young Billy.

He was face down in the water, arms open, caught in the V formed by the open driver's side door.

Unconscious.

"Stanley!" she shouted. "Help him!"

But Stanley couldn't stand. The log had become wedged in a large rock near the riverbank, and the edge of Stanley's coat had been caught on one of its many branches. He was twisting around madly, trying to unwind himself.

In the meantime, Jessica watched in horror as Young Billy's legs were caught by the stream. Slowly, his body was torn free from the vehicle. He began to slowly float down the river.

"The rope!" Jessica shouted. "Where's the rope?"

"Right here," Stanley shouted back. "He must've slipped out of it. Damnit, what is *wrong* with my coat?"

Without thinking, Jessica began following Young Billy. She was running alongside the creek, dodging brambles, ducking under branches, leaping over pools of rainwater, splashing through the ones that she couldn't—all while waiting for the opportunity to grab him.

Then it came.

He'd floated into an eddy near the bank. He'd been face-down for at least twenty seconds now. Jessica knew there wasn't much time left.

She leaped into the creek, not knowing or caring how deep or how strong the current was. She gasped as she plunged down to her waist and her boots scrambled for grip on the rocky bottom. The water was cold, much colder than it had any right to be.

Shivering, Jessica shivering turned over Young Billy's body. It wasn't easy to do, even when weightless in water, and she strained as she plunged her arms underwater, scooping him. When he was at last on his back, she hooked one arm underneath his armpit, and began to move the three steps back to the bank—

—when she heard a loud roar. She looked up. An enormous brown wave was rolling down the creek, seemingly as high as a mountain. Two words entered her mind.

Flash flood.

It occurred to Jessica that this was how she might die.

She had little time to prepare. She shut her eyes and hugged Young Billy tight, thinking about everything he'd done for her, everything Nonna had meant to her, how much she needed the farm, how much she'd wanted to show other people that she wanted it too.

Then she felt a wide lasso land around her shoulders.

Stanley was standing there on the riverbank, the other end of the rope in his hands.

"Put it around him too!"

She quickly draped it around them both. Arms around him, Jessica squeezed Young Billy.

With a quick yank, Stanley cinched it tight. She heard him shout, "Don't let go of—"

Then the wave hit, and Jessica lost herself in foam, froth, freezing water, and unconsciousness.

Chapter Forty-Eight

BEIGE.

It was blurry beige, a spinning wash of color, with hundreds of small squiggles slowly resolving themselves. At first Jessica thought she was still in the raging creek, or that she was dead.

"She's awake," said a voice.

Slowly Jessica realized that she was neither swimming nor dead. She was looking at a ceiling made of particle board. Her skin was touching cotton. It was a bedsheet. She was no longer in a swollen raging creek, or even outside—

She was on a bed.

Jessica flicked her eyes around the room. There was the IV drip. The visitor chairs. The television mounted on the wall.

This was a hospital room.

"Hello, dear," said the voice.

With great effort Jessica turned her head. Her grandmother was sitting on the chair next to her, shawl around her shoulders, hands folded on the knob of her good cane. Her steely eyes were suffused with a soft glow.

"Nonna."

"I have to say, this is quite the reversal."

"Is Young Billy—"

"He's fine," she answered. "You saved him."

"What happened to me?"

Nonna turned her head towards the door. "Stanley," she said.

The skinny farm manager walked in the door, hat in hand. In his eyes were a curious humor. Behind him walked Mary Kilkenny, pushing Richard in a wheelchair.

"Jessie," said Stanley.

"It's *Jessica*," she croaked.

He smiled. "I know."

"What the hell happened?"

"That damn creek sent you a hundred feet downriver. But you hung on to Young Billy, just like I told you to."

Jessica shifted. "I *told* you I could listen to directions."

"You did great." He smiled warmly. Jessica had never seen him do that before.

Mary cleared her throat. "You did good too, Stanley. You hauled both of them out of the river."

"And without your CPR," he replied, "they wouldn't have made it either."

Richard interrupted. "And don't forget Young Billy. He rescued us from our truck."

"Where is Young Billy?" said Jessica.

"Right here," said a voice.

Jessica turned her head. She hadn't noticed the curtain along one side of her room. Stanley swept it aside, revealing Young Billy laying in an identical bed, a black brace around his knee. In a nearby chair sat Ernesto, a microbiology textbook in his lap.

"Surprise," said Young Billy.

Jessica felt tears coming to her eyes. She reached out her arm. "I wish I could reach you."

He smiled. "You reached me just fine in that goddamned creek." He paused. "I owe you my life, Jessica."

"All right, goddamn it, that's enough," said Nonna. She stood up between them and swiped her cane in the air. "This is sounding like a Hollywood awards ceremony. I forbid any of you from giving any more credit to each other. You're *all* heroes today."

Nonna leaned over and kissed Jessica on the cheek. Then she kissed Young Billy on the cheek. Stanley presented his cheek. Nonna hesitated, then gave in, kissing him too.

Then Jessica noticed that someone had entered the doorway, a shadow of a person, her head bowed.

Her mother.

Nonna noticed too. "Look, Barbara's here," she said. Then she patted the chair next to her, closest to Jessica. "Come sit, dear."

Jessica's mother slipped quietly between the Kilkennys. She moved like someone who wanted to apologize for her own existence. She lowered herself onto the chair.

"Hi Barbara," said Jessica.

A tight little line that passed for a smile ran across her mother's face.

"We've had problems in our relationship," she said.

The assembled people were listening closely, and Jessica felt embarrassed. "Not here," she said.

"No," said her mother, "I want them to hear this too."

"Hear what?" said Jessica.

"That we can't be like this. I know that I haven't been the best mother, but I want to be in your life. I hope you want to be in mine."

"You hurt me," said Jessica, "over and over."

Tears appeared in her mother's eyes. "Well, I'm asking for your forgiveness." Then she sat back, her hands twisting each other like a pair of writhing snakes. "There, I said it. And everybody here heard me say it."

Jessica gulped. Her mother looked like an empty, crushed pack of cigarettes.

"Okay," she said.

Her mother let out a weird, choked cry—then flung her arms around Jessica. She managed to return it halfway.

They released each other, and her mother wiped the tears from her eyes. "You'll do anything for other people," she said. "You were always like that. I don't know where you get that from."

Jessica looked at Nonna. "I know where."

"What did I say earlier, Jessica?" said her grandmother. "This is a no-kiss-ass zone."

Jessica laughed. Then she sat up in bed and looked around, with clear eyes. "So I have a question."

"Yes, dear," said Nonna.

"When can I leave this hospital room and get back to the farm?"

Chapter Forty-Nine

AS THE SUN began to fall on Nonna's farm, Jessica strolled through the crowds of people, a name badge pinned proudly on her chest.

Jessica: Assistant Manager, Nonna's Farms.

It was their first Family Sunday.

Stanley had been as good as his word. After pinning down this particular Sunday in June—people were too busy on Saturdays with weddings—the staff of Nonna's Farms had spent four furious weeks planning the event. There had been township ordinances to learn, handicapped ramps to build, port-a-potties to rent, vendors to hire, a small stage to build, temporary corrals to erect, horseshoe pits to dig, advertisements to take out.

This morning, they'd opened the front gate at eight o'clock am this morning, expecting fifty cars at most.

To their surprise, over one hundred and twenty had arrived by noon. Richard Kilkenny, who'd been stationed alone at the front gate in his wheelchair to take admission, had finally abandoned the updates, too busy to text.

Jessica headed over to the crowd at the livestock demonstration. They were circled around Ernesto, who had brought two of the cattle in from the meadow. With the help of a wireless microphone clipped around his ear, he was giving a free class on livestock health.

In English.

Jessica had made sure of that. After the accident at the creek, she'd taken her newfound trust in Stanley to casually mention that their Mexican farmhand was definitely bilingual and possibly brilliant. That he was afraid of being fired if he didn't play illiterate and stupid. That this fear had been based on Stanley's previous behavior towards his Mexican farmhands.

"Is that what he thinks?" Stanley had said. "I fired Roberto for stealing. You tell Ernesto he can speak English any time he wants. Hell, I need all the bright ideas I can get around here."

Now, here at the livestock exhibition, Ernesto was giving all his bright ideas to the public. Jessica noticed the little girls who circled the ring, hanging on his every word. She also noticed some grown-up girls doing the same. In the middle of his lecture, Ernesto caught her eye and winked before continuing. Jessica saw several women swing their attention towards her.

She headed over to the farmhouse. Nonna was sitting on a rocking chair on the front porch, a group of twenty children at her feet. She was telling stories about the early days on the farm, gesturing out towards the orchard with her cane. This was *Storytime With Nonna*, and it had been Jessica's idea. Nonna had resisted at first. She had argued that nobody would want to listen to her.

From the way Nonna was excitedly acting out the story of her father's futile attempts to prevent the deer from eating his crops, though, Jessica could see that she was enjoying it. The tiny children were giggling.

Jessica's radio barked. It was Richard up front. "Jessica, it's four-thirty and I am closing the gates."

She radioed back: "What's the final vehicle count?"

"Two hundred thirteen."

Jessica stared at the radio in astonishment. Nonna had decided to charge by the vehicle, twenty dollars each, to encourage big families to attend. Jessica did the math in her head. They'd just made over four thousand dollars on admission alone. And since they'd spent a little over two thousand in preparations, this meant that they took home a tidy little profit.

There would be another Family Sunday.

She watched the cars beginning to pull out of the parking area, a hardened dirt area that had lain fallow for decades, used mostly for outdoor equipment storage during the summer. It was perfect for automobiles. She watched the line of gleaming metal trickle out of the parking area and down the road towards the exit, slowing down at the gate to receive their complimentary bag of produce, one per car. It'd been Young Billy's idea.

She walked over to the goat enclosure. A small crowd was sitting on the elevated bleachers, which had been rented from Hackmore's general store. Jessica had asked Tommy for the rental, and he'd thrown an extra day's rental for free. She suspected that he'd gotten the message.

In the enclosure, Young Billy was finishing a goat rodeo. He hadn't had to do much except set up a few rings and barrels, then get frustrated when the goats knocked over all the props and started to eat his own clothing. It was a farce, and Young Billy loved playing the clown. The children in the crowd loved it the most.

As the crowd climbed down from the bleachers, a woman with a small girl caught sight of Jessica. She came over. "Do you work here?" she said.

"I do."

"I have a question for you," she said. Jessica noticed that she was wearing heels and a cream-colored silk top. Her fingernails were elaborately styled with tiny rhinestones.

"I might have an answer," said Jessica.

She handed a piece of lavender paper at Jessica. "I drove eighty miles to see the farm that has such a beautiful sense of design. Who drew this?"

Jessica looked down and smiled. It was the flyer promoting this event, a woman's mass of hair that resolved into a cornucopia of fruits and vegetables. It'd been designed and hand-drawn by her city friend, Phineas. She'd called him to mend fences, so to speak; to her surprise, he'd apologized sincerely and asked to make it up to her. Jessica had made the request for artwork, and he'd leapt on it. Within a day, he'd returned four possible designs to her. All were gorgeous, and she'd had difficulty picking just one.

"A staffer at *Spretza* magazine," she said.

"Oh my God, I love *Spretza*," said the woman. "Do you read it?"

"Not anymore," said Jessica, a knowing smile on her face. Then she looked at the flyer again. She couldn't remember photocopying anything on lavender paper.

"Where did you find this flyer?"

"Some guy was handing them out last weekend."

"Where?"

"At my farmers' market."

Jessica crinkled her nose. She'd been in charge of all marketing, and she hadn't asked anybody to do anything like that, certainly not on lavender paper.

"What did he look like?"

"He was a little heavy, kind of funny. Everybody had a flyer at the market that day. He must've handed out hundreds."

Jessica was taken aback. This woman had just described

Mikey, but Jessica hadn't asked him for any help. In fact, she'd been too busy to even return his voicemail after her harrowing encounter with the swollen creek.

"Thank you," she said. "I hope you had a good time visiting us today."

"Oh we did," said the woman. Jessica noticed that she was grasping a little girl by the hand. "Serena absolutely loves it. I like the city too much to move out here, but she seems to be a natural country girl."

Jessica patted the girl on the head, and as she watched the mother walk away, she could understand that conflict. She had just navigated through it.

Then she looked back at the gate. Against the trail of cars leaving the farm was a single car coming up the road. Jessica frowned. Richard Kilkenny said that he'd closed the front gate.

As the truck grew nearer, Jessica recognized the driver.

It was Mikey.

He parked near the goat enclosure and hopped out, fanning his face. He was reddened and his hair was a sweaty mess. There were dark rings soaked into the armpits of his denim shirt.

"You," said Jessica, "are in trouble."

He pointed to his chest. "Me?"

"You were advertising this event without our permission."

Mikey placed his hands on his hips and played offended. "Jessica, that is *preposterous*. I am offended that you would even *accuse* me of such a heinous breach of trust."

Jessica played along. "You drove all the way to the city to hand out flyers last weekend."

"*Please,*" he said. "I would never do something so generous. In fact, I don't care if this farm lives or dies."

Jessica slid up to him and put her arms around her waist. "Thank you."

"Ma'am," he said, "you'd better be careful. My imaginary wife might see us."

"Don't worry," she replied, "my imaginary husband is out of town."

"Illicit love. We're terrible."

"Let's go out tonight."

"And take this public? You're crazy."

"I don't care."

"At least let me take a shower first. It's not easy handing out flyers all day in this heat."

Jessica grabbed his shirt and pulled him closer. "In the school of romance, you get an A for effort."

"That's the highest score I've ever gotten," he said.

"Well?"

"Well what?"

She lifted an eyebrow, moistened her lips.

"Oh."

He brought his face down to hers—and a moment later, Jessica found herself involved in a long, deep kiss. It was blissful and felt like an eternity.

When they finally pulled apart, Jessica regarded him, a small smile playing upon her lips. "Meet you at Chickadee's?"

"When?"

"Eight o'clock."

"Forget it. I'm too tired to meet a gorgeous girl at my favorite bar. And the making out would probably kill me."

She laughed. "I'll see you then."

As Jessica turned and walked back to the farmhouse, she wiped her forehead, and paused to stare at the setting sun.

She had found her place on the farm.

Plotworks Publishing

If you enjoyed this story, please leave a review at the place where you purchased it.

Then visit Plotworks Publishing to find other stories to enjoy!

Now turn the page for a sneak peek at another Finding Home title!

GIRL

seeking

BEACH

a finding home
novel

The lake hasn't
changed. But she has.

HANNAH DOVE

Girl Seeking Beach

Amanda maneuvered through the network of freeways. Past the industrial region south of the city, through a sliver of Indiana, and finally into the mitten-shaped peninsula.

The state of Michigan.

Ten million people strong, the northern parts of the state swelled up like a forest of ticks in the summer. The whole state was a summer wonderland, a jewel of the Midwest, with forests, lakes, and beaches dominating life. Tourists came by the thousands for days, weeks, months at a time.

Amanda knew the basics: Michigan bordered four of the five Great Lakes, each one a massive basin of freshwater that stretched hundreds of miles across and up to four hundred meters deep. Altogether, the entire system contained more than twenty percent of all existing freshwater in the world.

But Lake Batonkin wasn't one of the major ones. It was one of many smaller inland lakes that had been scraped out of the terrain by retreating glaciers thousands of years ago. This one was located square in the middle of the northern part of the mitten, in a slight depression flanked by forests and hills.

It was Amanda's childhood lake.

As she rolled off the highway, Amanda rolled her windows down and took in the fresh scent of pine. In an instant, she was pulled back to a simpler time. The memories came back unbidden. Her father. Her mother. Her siblings.

And Elsie.

The intrusive thought entered her mind without permission. Amanda pushed it out the door and focused on the road.

Then she saw the familiar sign: *Uncle Mark's Country Fresh Produce.* The market at the side of the road that she'd stopped at with her father, every summer.

She pulled the car over and, for the next few minutes, exchanged one sad memory for a slightly more bearable one.

Just after five o'clock, Amanda passed a road sign.

Welcome to Lake Batonkin. Population: 2417.

The two-lane road she'd been following, US-25, was the main thoroughfare. The town of Lake Batonkin was a long ribbon of buildings on either side of the road. The commercial zone stretched for nearly a mile, and a smaller side road, Fort Street, ran parallel with it. On the other side of Fort Street was the nearly defunct railroad tracks, which were only used by the cargo train from downstate. It rolled through town at exactly eleven-seventeen every Tuesday night.

Amanda found the Sunset Cottages quickly. She pulled down the short gravel driveway and parked in the visitor's spot. There were five cottages, each one a small concrete block house with screen door. They looked as if they probably dated from the nineteen-forties. A lot of the earliest structures up here were nearing a century old.

She looked around for an office, or a reception. There wasn't one. But her eye caught sight of a note stuffed in the door of cottage number three. She went over and pulled it out and read it.

Amanda, this is ALL YOURS!!!! Key is in lock. Come say hi!!! - Lily

That was the name of the proprietor. Just below the note, a key waited in the lock. Amanda turned the knob. The door popped open.

Inside, the cottage was a relic of beachgoing days past. It was a single large room with mid-century chair and coffee table. It also appeared to be a mid-century bed—the mattress should've been swapped out decades ago. On the other side of the room was a small vintage kitchenette that looked like it'd featured in a 1940s noir detective novel. It was clearly original to the cottage. A sliver of a tiny bathroom peeked through a door in the corner.

"Wow," she said, out loud to nobody.

Amanda set her suitcase down and removed her jacket. She spun around a few times, sniffed the air. It smelled like a musty antique shop. As a child, she'd been in old summer cottages like this, but they seemed normal. Today, this felt like a museum piece.

It hadn't changed. But she had.

She spent the next few minutes unpacking her clothes and stowing them in the small chintzy wartime dresser. The insides of the drawers carried that old scent of old cigarettes and tobacco.

Then she put on her swimsuit, a robin's-egg-blue one-piece. She looked at herself in the cracked mirror that hung on the door to the bathroom. She was nobody's prize, but she wasn't anybody's dealbreaker either. Though Amanda could be critical of her body—like most everybody she knew—she also knew when to put those voices back in the bottle and stow it away.

Amanda didn't define herself by her body, and she wouldn't let other people define her that way either. She was a full person, with a brain, and a heart, and a future.

Now she was going to dive into her past.

Lake Batonkin patiently waited for her to arrive. Its flat surface mirrored the dusk, with only a stray ripple disturbing the tranquility.

Amanda walked on the beach, feeling the cool evening sand between her toes. It was a good feeling. Her feet had missed the squeak of the sand.

She tossed her towel onto an Adirondack chair and walked up to the edge of the lake. Tiny waves lapped at her toenails. A smile crept onto her face and curled up there like a bashful child.

She bent down and picked up a small mussel. It was a simple purplish-brown shell, but this was the reason for her arrival. She felt it in her hands. These small little creatures, not even sentient, were massively destructive. They cost hundreds of millions of dollars in lost shipping.

She tossed the thing backwards, away from the water. Tomorrow she'd start the investigation. Right now was for relaxation.

She slowly entered the lake. The water was still warm from the heat of the day; the thermal layer wouldn't dissipate until much later.

Amanda waded in up to her thighs, then made the decision to dive. It was always better to get in all at once. She closed her eyes, pressed her hands together, and dove in headfirst. The water sluiced cool around her cheeks and shoulders.

She came up with a short gasp, but not because she couldn't breathe. It was from happiness. More than a decade had passed since she'd been in these waters, and it felt like no time at all. She swam out over her head, which took a minute, then turned around. Treading water, she looked back at the shoreline.

Just beyond the beachline, a furze of oaks, maples, willows, and pines edged the perimeter of the lake, punctuated by large lakefront homes and the occasional lawn. Further down, she could make out the public beachfront promenade in downtown Lake Batonkin.

She felt her heart leap in her chest. Something about this place made Amanda feel alive.

She turned and looked the other way. Down the beach in the other direction was a small promontory.

Her heart suddenly plunged back down.

Amanda knew that promontory. She knew what had happened there. And she didn't want to revisit it.

Amanda swam back to shore and got out of the lake and wrapped a towel around her body. Then she sat down in the Adirondack chair and leaned over her knees, her fingers pressed to the bridge of her nose, eyes closed, waiting for the bad feelings to pass.

When they finally did, she rose to her feet and walked back to the cottage.

Plotworks Publishing

Turn the page for another sneak peek into a Hannah Dove cozy mystery! If you enjoy pet bunnies, baking, and murder, this story is for you—

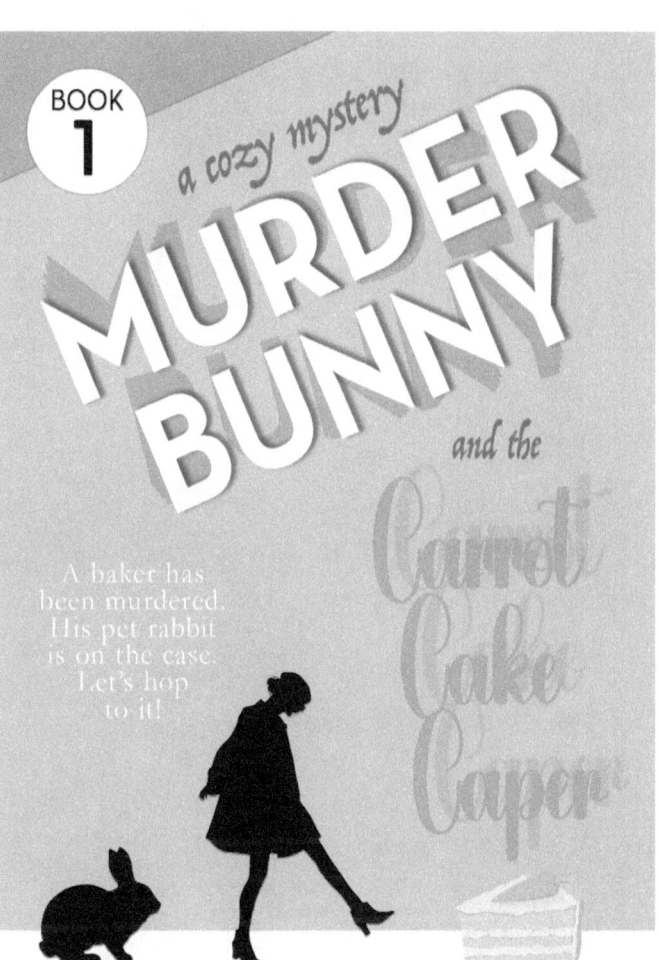

BOOK
1

a cozy mystery

MURDER BUNNY

and the

Carrot Cake Caper

A baker has
been murdered.
His pet rabbit
is on the case.
Let's hop
to it!

HANNAH DOVE

AUTHOR OF THE STEAMBOAT WILLIE WHISTLESTOP PUZZLE MYSTERIES

Murder Bunny and the Carrot Cake Caper

Goodness gracious, this day has been horrific. Yet it started out so positively that I can't quite make heads or tails of it.

I saw Nigel, my now-dead owner, wake up this morning feeling very enthusiastic about the qualifier round of the baking competition.

I watched him closely, as is my habit. He paced around the kitchen in his lavender terry cloth bathrobe, a mud mask on his face, going on and on about how he was certain to sail through the qualifier, about how the world wasn't ready for his newest recipe. He was right. Nobody was ready for that recipe. Nigel had come up with the greatest carrot cake that I'd ever nibbled.

And that's saying a lot, since I'm a bunny.

Anyways, Nigel carried on and on about cream cheese frosting, commitment to one's art, and how the most precious commodity in this world was enthusiasm. Nigel was always rambling on like that. He loved to address me, asking questions and then answering them. As usual I said nothing. I've found it's better to play stupid in the company of humans.

Everybody wants a dumb bunny.

Anyways, he was all a bit too much for me. As the rant continued, I hunched down in the corner of my hutch, nibbling on my morning watercress and scented lemon water, listening. The one good thing I will say about Nigel is that he always kept me stocked in the very best food and beverage.

I shall miss that about him.

At noon he emerged from his bedroom fully dressed in his white baker's outfit. I ran circles around the hutch for a few seconds, pretending to be excited. We have to embarrass ourselves, us bunnies, to keep a roof over our heads.

"Fluffy, if you continue behaving yourself, someday I'll let you inside my bedroom." He crouched down and peered at me. I could see the cream glistening on his mustache. "But until then, it's not for animals–no matter how cute." His finger jabbed at me through the squares of the cage, and my nose twitched involuntarily. I hate it when that happens.

It's both funny and sad that Nigel assumed I'd never seen his bedroom. Even given his posh British accent, with his plummy vowels and endless wit, he never figured out that I could open my cage. He never noticed the bits of pine shavings that I inevitably tracked out when I went out for my late-night adventures in his home. Maybe he'd mistaken me for a silly Pomeranian. That's fine.

Again, everybody wants a dumb bunny. So that's what I give them.

Nigel removed his recipe book from the cupboard and lay it gingerly upon the table. The recipe book had a combination lock on it, if you can believe that. He only opened it when nobody was around, and kept it locked and shelved at all other times.

Of course, I'd sussed out the four-digit combination long ago. You never know when you might need to know something like that.

I watched him lay the book out on the countertop and dial the combination and open it up.

"And so it begins," he announced to nobody. I watched him begin to assemble the ingredients. Flour, sugar, butter, eggs, carrots, vanilla essence. A series of unmarked containers with mysterious ingredients that his pudgy fingers handled with reverence. It was all a mystery to me.

But I had faith in Nigel. He'd worked for months on this carrot cake recipe, and he had the track record to prove it.

Next, he pulled the black cover from his red KitchenAid mixer and ran a loving finger along its edge. Nigel guarded the machine like a national treasure and spent his evenings cleaning it.

I curled up in my wood shavings and started to read the paper. You humans assume I can't read because I'm a bunny, but what you don't realize is that I've spent most of my life living on top of newspapers. They line the bottom of my cage, beneath the pine shavings, and I've learned about everything that you can learn from a newspaper, from news to sports to politics to lifestyle to weather to advertisements.

Nigel started the mixing, using both hand and machine. "See, Fluffy, what they don't know is that the texture starts at the beginning. It's the combination of the two." Later, he lovingly poured the batter into three different cake pans and massaged them with his silicone spatula. He slid the pans into the preheated oven and paced the kitchen while it baked, the sweet aroma of ginger and carrot floating through the air.

When the kitchen timer rang, Nigel sprang towards the oven. He removed the cakes, let them cool for exactly six minutes on the counter. Then he began assembling the finished product, handling the disks with great care, gently smoothing the cream cheese frosting between the layers, and finally coating the entire cake.

When it was finished, he removed a small box from a

cupboard. He opened it and gingerly removed a small bell tower, only a few inches high. "See this, Fluffy?" Nigel said. "It came into my store almost a year ago. It is the *perfect* topper. This is going to win me a sixth title."

He gently placed the bell tower on top of the cake. Then he backed away, rubbed his hands together, and giggled.

"I am the best," he said.

I twitched a skeptical whisker.

"What? It's not bragging if it's true."

Half an hour later, the cake was boxed up and in Nigel's car. He had put on his trenchcoat and begun humming to himself. I didn't know his intention, but I wasn't going to let him leave without me. I'd traveled with him to the fair each of the last five years. I'd suffered the fingers of pink frosting thrust into my hutch, the bits of oatmeal cookie that children dropped onto my back from above.

Spending a week at the county fair wasn't my cup of tea, but I refused to be left alone. He didn't know it, but Nigel needed me.

Drawing in my breath, I stood up on my hind legs, gripped my cage with my paws, and rattled it using every ounce of my strength.

Nigel stopped in the doorway and turned. "What's that, Fluffy? You want to come?"

Fluffy. The name made me nauseated. I never liked that diminutive. Still, I began leaping, just to make my intentions clear.

"Well, that's a surprise." He stroked his chin. "I thought that you didn't enjoy the fair last year."

I shook the cage harder, then did a cute flip.

Nigel sighed. "All right, I suppose you could come this year." He picked up my crate by the handle and carried me outside.

I was quite fond of Nigel. He usually did what I wanted.

———

At the fair, Nigel got a couple of the local kids to set up the tent in exchange for some biscuits he'd made. He wasn't going to waste his carrot cake on them. Wise. Children have no appreciation for good food. Sticky little creatures think anything with enough sugar is delicious.

Nigel rested my hutch down in the corner of the tent and began setting up his cake station in the center. Today was all about flavor, but Nigel was a showman. He'd brought a stand and the belltower and even a set of tiny lights. He loved a good presentation and said that it was the reason for his win.

One by one, people trickled over while he was preparing his cake. I recognized a few of them. They'd be competing with Nigel in the contest. A lot of them offered him some of their own foods to try. I could tell from the look of triumph on his face and the condescending compliments that none of their desserts could approach the magnificence of Nigel's carrot cake.

As they chatted, I lay in my hutch, watching their feet and waiting for the cooing to begin. Sure enough, it did. *Oh my look at him.* Then: *What a beautiful little creature!* Finally: *Be careful or he might end up on my plate!* I twitched my whiskers and pretended to giggle at that one. You have no idea how many times I've been sweetly threatened to end up on somebody's plate.

The crowd died down. The occasional person would come in and speak with Nigel, but I paid it little attention. There was a lump of frosting stuck on my ear. No amount of scratching with my paw seemed to be getting it off. It was driving me crazy and keeping me quite preoccupied.

That's when I heard a thump, and then a cry.

Nigel had fallen over, onto the ground. I couldn't see his face but something was definitely wrong. I don't know if he was breathing or not.

I wondered if I ought to break out of my cage and go for help, but I saw another pair of feet. There was another human in the tent. I assumed they would sound an alarm or call for help of some kind, whatever it was humans did when someone suddenly fell to the floor clutching their chest.

The feet vanished, and I waited. Surely, someone would come soon.

It was a few minutes before another pair of feet appeared. I heard a girl calling Nigel's name. She screamed.

The next hour was a flurry of activity. I saw legs, calves, and feet, but I couldn't see Nigel through the crowd. I heard the anxious voices conferring closely. By the time the paramedics arrived, I began running in frantic circles in my cage, but nobody noticed me. Dumb bunnies get forgotten. I watched them put Nigel on a stretcher and wheel him away.

Then a pair of black police shoes arrived next to my cage. "We'll have to take this bunny to a shelter of some kind," said a male voice. "It doesn't seem like Nigel has anyone in the area to take him."

"A shelter?" said another voice. "Could as well just let him free, y'know? The shelter's only going to end up putting him down."

My ears went flat. I felt the panic rising in my haunches. Did I get a say between those two options? Because I definitely chose freedom. I began to run in circles trying to communicate this choice. I didn't know what else to do. Sometimes it worked, sometimes it didn't.

They weren't looking at me.

"Don't say that," the first man said. "He'll be fine. The animal shelter's not that bad."

Then my cage was lifted up. I saw the humans. They didn't stare at me like I was used to, however. They were too busy examining the tent. I looked around and spotted Nigel's display table. The lighting, the decorations, and the cake stand were all there.

However, the carrot cake that Nigel had spent the morning obsessing over had vanished.

The officer kept carrying my crate, taking me out of the tent. I didn't have time to dwell on the missing cake.

I could feel my heart thumping. This was very bad. I had to deal with one problem at a time. I couldn't survive in an animal shelter. They'd toss me in a little crate with a bunch of other rabbits. They'd feed me pellets. I'd have to tolerate the dumb bunnies' dumb conversation. It would be torture.

In the midst of my panic, I gazed out at the crowd of humans around Nigel's tent. That was when I saw her.

A young woman wearing a conservative yellow gingham print dress. It had a ruff around the neck. Her dark hair was cut in a conservative bob and her fingers were interlaced around a small clutch. Her eyes were large and sensitive and even a little watery. She looked like someone who needed a bunny.

And she was looking at me.

I had to act fast. I flipped my body around and kicked open the cage door. I knew exactly how to make it look like an accident. Then I leaped out onto the ground and hopped straight over to the woman. I sat on her shoe and leaned my head against her shin and began trembling.

"Oh my goodness," she said.

"He likes you, Agnes," said the police officer. He came over and looked down at me. I was really shivering now. It wasn't easy to look this vulnerable but I knew that my future depended upon it.

"I'm unsure about what to do."

"Agnes, would you be willing to take care of Nigel's bunny for a while?" he said.

She looked down at me. I looked up at her. Our eyes met.

"Yes, I suppose I will," she replied.

Plotworks Publishing

Now turn the page to discover the world of Castor's Grove! Orphan's Egg is a sweet paranormal romance by A.J. Renwick—

CASTOR'S GROVE

ORPHAN'S EGG

a young adult paranormal romance

A.J. RENWICK

Orphan's Egg

Frances West stood, frozen on the sidewalk, staring at the familiar gray door.

It was the first thing she'd recognized since returning to Castor's Grove three weeks ago. Though she'd been born in the city, Fran's time in it had felt less like a homecoming than she'd secretly hoped. The streets were easy to navigate with buildings organized in square grids, her temporary apartment on the edge of downtown was clean and conveniently located, and there was nothing lacking in the environment. With the ocean on its south and east borders, forest to the north and west, and dense urban high-rises in its center, Castor's Grove was a city that boasted something for everyone.

But there was nothing special about a city that everyone could enjoy. Fran liked it, but it was in the same way any visitor might. While waiting to hear back from the adoption agency, she'd wandered the streets, avoiding the usual tourist activities, waiting to see something that sparked some long-buried memory or wander into someone who would recognize her.

Now, it was happening.

But instead of the sense of belonging she'd imagined, Fran's chest tightened, and her breath caught. Her anxiety buzzed in her brain.

There was an image of a sword burned into the door. It stretched almost the entire length of the door, its hilt hovering only a few inches above a sunflower welcome mat that looked far too normal in the context. Who lived in this house?

Your foster parents. Fran grappled with her anxiety to take control of her own thoughts. *They're probably into Dungeons and Dragons, or one of the kids they cared for did it.*

Either way, it was nothing to worry about.

Fran took a deep breath and pushed her hands into the pocket of her large black jacket. It wasn't cold, but she wrapped it around her as she walked up the steps. There was no doorbell. She tapped her elbow against the wood.

No response came from within. Fran could've tried again. It had been a light knock.

This is too weird. They might not even live here anymore. What was I thinking just knocking on their door?

She should just leave a message. There was paper in her pocket; she could buy a pen somewhere nearby, write a letter, and slip it into the mailbox.

"Upon my honor."

Fran spun around to see a thin middle-aged woman with olive skin. Short gray hairs frizzed around her temples, narrowly escaping the band that pulled the rest into a black ponytail. She wore an oversized green dress with a canary yellow jacket that matched the shopping bag in her hand.

The woman took a few steps closer, keeping her eyes on Fran. There was a wariness to her expression.

"Um, I was just—"

There was nothing suspicious about knocking on someone's door in broad daylight, but Fran felt suddenly guilty. "Do you know if the Franklins still live here?"

"We do." She narrowed her eyes, glancing between Fran and the door as though she thought the teenager was blocking her path. "Is this a university project? Are you doing a census?"

Fran was tempted to lie, tell Mrs. Franklin yes, and bolt, but she'd made it this far, so she shook her head. "No, I'm not with the university. I'm actually, well I was, one of the kids you fostered. It was like fifteen years ago. You probably don't remember—"

"Frances Buckler."

The sound of her original name rang like a bell in Fran's ears. Her lips mouthed the word *Buckler*, trying to wrap themselves around the harsh first syllable and the slur of the second. She'd whispered it to herself every night since she'd learned it, but it still felt like it belonged to someone else.

"It's Frances West now, actually."

"You've dyed your hair." Mrs. Franklin reached toward her, and Fran flinched away, but she was too slow to stop the woman from grabbing a clump of black hair. She ran a finger along it as though testing if the dye would rub off. Then she dropped the hair, pulled a set of keys out from her bag, and turned to the door. "Come inside. You shouldn't be out here."

"Oh." Fran pulled her jacket tight again. Her first instinct was to refuse. Stranger danger and all that. But how did she expect to get information about her parents if she didn't talk to Mrs. Franklin? "Maybe for a minute, but I can't stay long."

The strange yet familiar door led to a normal and therefore relatively forgettable living area. There was a fireplace in the corner with olive green couches and a squat brown coffee table. Paintings of flowers hung on the walls.

Fran's stomach tightened as she stepped in. *Why doesn't it match the door?*

"Sit." Mrs. Franklin instructed, pointing at the couch.

Fran hesitated, but the woman kept smiling and staring.

Eventually, she gave in and sat on the edge of one of the chairs. Mrs. Franklin didn't join her.

"You must tell me about your life, dear. What's brought you back to the city?"

"Nothing in particular," Fran said, fingers crumpling stray pieces of paper in her pockets as she tried to guess what Mrs. Franklin's angle was.

There's no angle. She's just a nice older lady who took care of me for six months when I was a toddler. Don't listen to your anxiety.

"Although, I was wondering if you knew anything about my parents," Fran forced the truth out. "I wouldn't bother you about it, but there's no record of them anywhere, no birth certificate on file for me, but you're the one who recorded my last name as Buckler, and my dads said you sent that gift with me, so I just thought, maybe you'd known them?"

Fran held her breath as she waited for Mrs. Franklin's response. This was it. Her former foster parents were her last chance of learning the truth about her birth parents. Who had they been? What had they done? Had they loved her?

The woman before her might have those answers.

Mrs. Franklin's smile faltered. "What gift?"

"You know," Fran said. If the woman had been able to recognize Frances after fifteen years, she must have remembered it. "The Fabergé egg. It's purple with gold details."

Mrs. Franklin's smile stretched so tight that it looked like her skin would snap. "You still have that?"

"Obviously." Sarcasm leaked into Fran's voice before she could stop it. Did the woman really think she'd have thrown away the only gift she'd ever received from her parents?

"It's here with you? In the city?"

Fran stiffened, feeling her heart thump in her chest. That was a strange question. It wasn't just her paranoia.

"No. I left it back in Lansing."

"Excuse me a moment. I need to make a call." Mrs. Franklin spoke with the smile frozen on her face.

Fran nodded. Her eyes flicked to the front door. It was close, but not so close that the older woman couldn't grab her before she got to it.

Mrs. Franklin didn't leave the room. Eyes trained on Frances, she pulled a phone from her pocket, pressed a button, and raised it to her ear.

Fran struggled to keep her breathing steady as she stared at the woman.

"Dammit." Mrs. Franklin's smile finally dropped as she lowered the phone. She knelt on the carpeted floor before Fran and rested her hands on the teenager's knees.

Fran was small, but the woman before her was frail. She could push her off. But her body was frozen. All she could think about was the fact that she should've hidden her knife in her pocket instead of her boot.

"Listen, Frances, I have the answers you want, okay? But we need to be honest with one another. What's the address of your home in Lansing?"

There was no way Fran was telling her that.

"Never mind. Two dads, West? I'll look it up. Just wait here until I'm back, okay? I'll tell you about your parents then."

Before Fran could fully process what the woman had said, Mrs. Franklin had raced out of her own house. The tension in Fran's body slackened as she realized that she was alone, but her heart continued to quiver. This was all far too weird, and try as she might, Fran couldn't pierce through her anxiety to come up with a logical reason for Mrs. Franklin's actions.

I need to leave.

But Mrs. Franklin knew her parents. Fran could finally learn who they were, who she was.

The longing burned within her, begged her to stay, just as

her anxiety screamed at her to run. The result was that Fran sat on the olive chair for a lot longer than most sane people would have. And she might have remained there until Mrs. Franklin returned were it not for the noise.

A loud twang shook the floor beneath Fran's chair.

That settled it. She leaped up and grabbed the door handle without hesitation. But it wouldn't budge. Mrs. Franklin had locked her in.

Crap.

Trustworthy people didn't lock teenagers in their houses. Whatever claims Mrs. Franklin made about her parents could easily be false. She couldn't stick around.

But how could she escape?

The Franklins' house had only one entry, and there were bars on all their windows. Except for the ones in the basement.

It was the design of all the houses in this area. Fran had noticed it while walking through the neighborhood. But the strange noise had come from the basement.

Fran reached into her boot and pulled out her knife. Fingers trembling, she managed to get the blade free. She held it before her, afraid to breathe as she searched for the basement door.

It didn't take her long to find it in the kitchen.

Cold sweat trickled down Fran's back as she stared down a long flight of steps. There was no sound now save Fran's own pounding heart.

Maybe the noise she'd heard was a cat. People owned those. They knocked things over. At least, they did in television shows.

And I think I'm too smart to die in a horror movie? This is the dumbest thing I've ever done.

But waiting for Mrs. Franklin would've been just as foolish. So Fran tiptoed down the stairs, knuckles white around her knife.

A stream of light from a high window illuminated the bottom of the staircase. The tension eased from Fran's body. It was too high for her to climb through, but there might be a ladder or something she could stand on down below. Maybe she wasn't about to die.

"Dust!" a boy's voice exclaimed.

Or maybe she was.

"Couldn't you at least give me a few minutes to try to escape? Maybe we could make a trade?"

Fran's legs turned into metal rods, anchored to the ground, unable to move. Her heart did its best to escape them. It took all her effort to turn her head toward the voice.

Her mouth dropped open. The only thing that stopped her from gasping was that her chest was too tight to let the breath escape.

Trapped underneath a silver net was a boy about her own age with a mass of red curls. But it wasn't the net or the color of his hair that made Fran feel as though she were about to faint.

He had wings.

Plotworks Publishing

Be sure to visit our store at Plotworks Publishing to discover even more titles to enjoy!